Two Strange Tales

Two Strange Tales

Mircea Eliade

Shambhala
Boston & London
1986

SHAMBHALA PUBLICATIONS, INC.
Horticultural Hall
300 Massachusetts Avenue
Boston, Massachusetts 02115
www.shambhala.com

Printed in the United States of America

Distributed in the United States by Random House, Inc., and in Canada by Random House of Canada Ltd

LIBRARY OF CONGRESS CATALOGING-IN-PUBLICATION DATA

Eliade, Mircea, 1907–1986.
    Two strange tales.
    Consists of Nights at Serampore, translation of Nopti la Serampore, and The secret of Dr. Honigberger, translation of Secretul doctorului Honigberger.
    ISBN 1-57062-663-4 (pbk.)
    I. Eliade, Mircea, 1907–1986. Secretul doctorului Honigberger. English. 1986. II. Title.
PC839.E38N6513   1986   86-13026
859'.334

BVG 01

CONTENTS

Introduction, by the Author   vii

Nights at Serampore   1

The Secret of Dr. Honigberger   61

v

INTRODUCTION

BY THE AUTHOR

IT may seem presumptuous for an author to write an introduction to the translation of one of his older books, but I do not see how I can otherwise avoid some misunderstanding. It is by sheer chance that *Two Tales of the Occult* is the first to appear in English.[1] It so happened that a few years ago Professor W. A. Coates found *Nächte in Serampore*[2] in a bookshop in Frankfurt, and after reading the two tales wanted to compare the German and French translations with the original version in Rumanian. He then proceeded to learn Rumanian and eventually decided to retranslate them from the original tongue. If these stories were my only literary work, the most characteristic, or

1. Eric Tappe has recently published the Rumanian text with a parallel English translation of two short stories: "Twelve Thousand Head of Cattle" and "A Great Man" in *Fantastic Tales* (London, Dillon, 1969, pp. 10–75).

2. Translation of *Secretul Doctorului Honigberger* and *Nopti la Serampore* by Günther Spaltmann (Otto-Wilhelm-Barth-Verlag, Munich-Planegg 1953). Cf. also *Minuit à Serampore*, translated from the German by Albert-Marie Schmidt (Paris Librairie Stock, 1956).

even the most recent, I would not have felt obligated to add the present preface. But these novelettes, written in 1939–40, represent only a fragment of my literary *oeuvre* which includes, among other miscellaneous writings, some ten novels and three volumes of short stories. Only a few of these works belong to what is usually called *littérature fantastique*. Besides this, even though the present *Tales of the Occult* are generally characteristic, they can hardly be said to be representative of my other writings in this genre. Before and especially after 1940, I have been attracted to other themes and have experimented with different literary techniques.

I do realize, of course, how difficult it is adequately to discuss a literary corpus only partially translated into French, German, Spanish, and other languages, but entirely inaccessible to the reader of English. I am partly responsible for this situation, since I did not do anything to promote the English translations of my literary writings. I was preoccupied with other works, especially the completion of a number of books on Indian philosophy and the history of religions which, from 1945 on, I was writing in French. Without Mr. Coates' initiative, even the present volume would not have appeared. For I could not decide how a rather large and complex literary production should best be introduced to the English-reading public. Understandably, I preferred to see translated first of all *Forêt Interdite* (Gallimard, 1955), the novel I consider my chef-d'oeuvre. But what publisher would undertake the risk of bringing out a 640-page novel written by an author primarily known as an historian of religions? Consequently, I abandoned the immediate possibility of publishing English translations of my literary works to the fates of some more favorable future. Meanwhile, I continued to write fiction in Rumanian, even though for many years my only readers were my wife and a few friends. But this is another story . . .

I shall not try to discuss here the relation of my *littérature fantastique* to the rest of my literary production.[3] But I would like to say something with regard to the present *Tales of the Occult.* I think it will be evident to any attentive reader that I wanted to relate some yogic techniques, and particularly yogic folklore, to a series of events narrated in the literary genre of a mystery story. In both novelettes a number of important personages are real. Dr. J. M. Honigberger is still remembered today for his book *Thirty-five Years in the East* (London, 1852). Among the characters in "Nights at Serampore," the Tibetan scholar, Johan van Manen, and the learned Islamicist, Lucian Bogdanof, were both well known in the cultural milieux of Calcutta during the period between the two Wars; and, as for Swami Shivananda, I lived near him for the six months of my stay in a Himalayan ashram at Rishi Kesh, and later, after 1935, he became tremendously popular all over India (he is the author of some 400 books and pamphlets on Vedanta, Yoga, and almost everything else).

However, throughout these two tales I have carefully introduced a number of imaginary details, in order to awaken in any cautious reader suspicion concerning the authenticity of the yogic "secrets." For instance, at a certain moment the life of Dr. Honigberger is radically mythologized, as one can see from any of his biographies.[4] Likewise, the region around Seram-

3. The interested reader may find some insights in the contributions of Virgil Ierunca ("The Literary Work of Mircea Eliade"), Günther Spaltmann ("Authenticity and Experience of Time: Remarks on Mircea Eliade's Literary Works"), Vintila Horia ("The Forest as Mandala: Notes Concerning a Novel by Mircea Eliade"), George Uscatescu ("Time and Destiny in the Novels of Mircea Eliade") in Joseph M. Kitagawa and Charles H. Long, ed., *Myths and Symbols: Studies in Honor of Mircea Eliade* (Chicago, University of Chicago Press, 1969, pp. 343–406).

4. See, for instance, the competent article by Arion Rosu in *Zeitschrift der deutschen morgenländischen Gesellschaft,* 1967.

pore is described in such a way as to reveal its status as a mythical geography. The same observation is pertinent with regard to certain of the yogic techniques depicted: some descriptions correspond to real experiences, but others reflect more directly yogic folklore. As a matter of fact, this *mélange* of reality and fiction is admirably suited to the writer's central conception of "camouflage" as a dialectical moment. (I may recall that any hierophany reveals the *sacred* hidden in a *profane* object or entity.) But in these two stories "camouflage" is used in a paradoxical manner, for the reader has no means to decide whether the "reality" is hidden in "fiction," or the other way around, because both processes are intermingled.

I will not elaborate any further concerning the literary technique of these two stories. It suffices to add that I knowingly utilized a number of clichés, for my ambition was to follow as closely as possible the popular models of the genre, while introducing into the narrative the dialectic of camouflage. But, as I already indicated, while "The Secret of Dr. Honigberger" and "Nights at Serampore" are characteristic, neither is fully representative of my *littérature fantastique*. In my other stories in the fantastic vein I have utilized the dialectic of camouflage in different ways. It is pointless to give examples, since it is almost impossible to analyze stylistically various types of fantastic tales within the confines of a simple *résumé*. In fact, I even doubt whether such tales can be really summarized, their literary qualities and their "mystery" residing precisely in the experienced texture of the narrative. I can only say that, besides employing different stylistic approaches, I have repeatedly taken up the themes of *"sortie du Temp,"* and of the alteration, or the transmutation, of space in a number of stories. A favorite technique of mine aims at the imperceptible yet gradual transmutation of a commonplace setting into a new "world," without however losing its proper, everyday, or "natural" structure and qualities. In a short novel, *Sarpele*, written and published in 1937,[5] a rather ordinary picnic in the vicinity of a monastery is transformed unwittingly into a strange ritual after the unexpected appearance of a snake. But the "fantastic" atmosphere unfolds almost "naturally," and not a single supernatural element intervenes to destroy the familiar world of a depressingly banal group of townspeople enjoying their picnic. The "parallel world" of the fantastic is indistinguishable from the given, ordinary world, but once this other world is discovered by the various characters it blurs, changes, transforms, or dislocates their lives in different ways.

In "La Tigănci" ("With the Gypsies"[6]), a mediocre, absent-minded piano teacher pauses by chance one very hot afternoon in front of a curious house, where upon meeting a young girl he is lured into seeing "the gypsies." A series of strange incidents and rather childish games follow; but when, a few hours later, the piano teacher leaves the house he gradually discovers that something is wrong—the town, his house, and his acquaintances have all changed. He is told—but he does not believe—that twelve years have passed while he was involved in the innocent, almost meaningless adventures in the "gypsies'" house.

In a somewhat similar way, *Pe strada Mântuleasa* (1968), recently translated by Eric Tappe but not yet published, relates the tale of the intrusion of the bizarre personal memories of an old man on the official bureaucratic world. In this story the style becomes a counterpoint to the narrative which depicts the encounter of two different, antagonistic, and yet finally identical

5. Translated into German by Günther Spaltmann: *Andronic und die Schlange* (Munich, Nymphenburger Verlag, 1949).

6. Translated into French by Allain Guillermou: "Les Bohémiennes" (*La Revue de Paris*, Décembre 1966, pp. 29-58).

mythological worlds. In an attempt to explain himself to the city officials, the old man, Fărâmă, becomes involved in writing out a long, rambling, and hopelessly labyrinthian history of his earlier experiences and memories as headmaster of the primary school in Strada Mântuleasa—an account that seems to be more legend and folklore than history to the officials. In the frustrating process of interrogation the two worlds gradually impinge and merge, and the bureaucratic world begins to function fantastically.

In all of these more recent stories, the "fantastic" elements disclose, or more precisely create, a series of "parallel worlds" which do not pretend to be "symbols" of something else. Thus, it is fruitless to read into the events and characters of the stories a hidden meaning that may illuminate certain aspects of immediate reality. Each tale creates its own proper universe, and the creation of such imaginary universes through literary means can be compared with mythical processes. For any myth relates a story or tale of a creation, tells how something came into being—the world, life, or animals, man, and social institutions. In this sense, one can speak of a certain continuity between myth and literary fiction, since the one as well as the other recounts the creation (or the "revelation") of a universe parallel to the everyday world. Of course, myth has also an exemplary value in traditional or primitive societies, and this is no more true for literary works. One must keep in mind, however, that a literary creation can likewise reveal unexpected and forgotten meanings even to a contemporary, sophisticated reader.

This is not the place to expand such considerations of the function and significance of *littérature fantastique*. I want only to suggest that such types of literary creativity may also constitute authentic instruments of knowledge. The imaginary universes brought to light in *littérature fantastique* disclose some dimensions of reality that are inaccessible to other intellectual approaches. But certainly, it is not for this reason that most authors write "fantastic" proses; at least, this is not the case for me. But any work of fiction reveals a method aiming at a specific type of knowledge. The methodological implications of *littérature fantastique* are still to be elucidated and systematized. For an historian of religions, trying to clarify and improve his own method, this opens an intriguing problem. Actually, the historian of religions in the same way as the writer of fiction is constantly confronted with different structures of (sacred and mythological) space, different qualities of time, and more specifically by a considerable number of strange, unfamiliar, and enigmatic worlds of meaning.

For some time now the literary critics have successfully used the findings of historians of religions in their hermeneutics. Unfortunately, this is not the case with the majority of the historians of religions; they still have some puritanical or bourgeois prejudices against literature,[7] thus neglecting or ignoring the tremendous work done in the last twenty years by literary critics and theoreticians. Ironically, it was precisely in such efforts to analyze and elucidate the structures, modalities, and meanings of literary universes, that historians of religions could have found the help or inspiration they vainly sought in sociology, anthropology, or psychology.

I am grateful to Professor Coates that, thanks to his enthusiasm, I have had the opportunity to touch on an aspect of my writing which for a long time I have almost kept as a secret.

---

7. They are not alone. Professor Ayer thought that he could not better discredit Jean-Paul Sartre and the existentialist philosophy than by entitling his devastating critique: "Philosophers-Novelists."

Nights at Serampore

1.

Never shall I forget the nights which I spent in the company of Bogdanof and Van Manen in the environs of Calcutta, at Serampore and Titagarh. Bogdanof, who had spent ten years as Consul of the Czarist Empire in Teheran and Kabul, had undertaken to teach me Persian. We had become friends, despite the differences in age and intellectual standing—for he was a noted Orientalist and contributor to the most celebrated journals, while I was still a very young student—mainly because we both belonged to the Orthodox Church. Bogdanof had remained true to his Orthodox faith both among the Moslems of Persia and Afghanistan, for whom he had a great love, and among the Hindus of Bengal, for whom he felt an aversion he was scarcely able to conceal. Van Manen, on the other hand, all but worshipped everything Indian. He had for many years been librarian and secretary of the Asiatic Society of Bengal, and before that he had for a time been librarian of the Theosophical Society at Adyar. He was a Dutchman in the second half of life, who had come to India in early youth, and, like so many

3

others, had succumbed to its charms for good. He had devoted some twenty-five years to the study of the Tibetan language, and had a better understanding of it than anyone else; however, he was lazy and enjoyed good living, so he had published very little. He was content to study and increase his knowledge purely for his own enjoyment. He had not the slightest respect for academic titles; he was a bachelor; and he had an inclination —which he kept secret—towards the occult.

As soon as the rainy season was over and the days became a bit cooler, we were inseparable. All three of us used to work in the library of the Asiatic Society on Park Street, Bogdanof and I at the same table, Van Manen in his office. Bogdanof was revising a translation of Mohammed Dhara Shikuh and Van Manen was cataloguing some Tibetan manuscripts which had recently been purchased in Sikkim, while I was struggling with the *Subhāshita Samgraha,* a text which is well known for its extreme difficulty. Each of us respected the other's devotion to his task, and except for a few words exchanged between Bogdanof and myself when we raised our eyes from the pages before us to light a cigarette, we hardly spoke. But a few minutes before the library closed, the three of us would meet in Van Manen's office, and there our long conversations would begin, which sometimes went on until long after midnight.

The Calcutta nights, especially in mid-autumn, are indescribably beautiful. There is nothing I can compare them to. In their atmosphere the melancholy of the Mediterranean night and the melodiousness of the northern night are fused with that sensation of dissolving into nothingness which is instilled in the soul by the night of the oriental seas and those overpowering scents of plant life that meet you as soon as you penetrate into the heart of India. For me especially these nights were suffused with a magic which I was utterly unable to withstand. Often,

4

even before I made the acquaintance of the two illustrious scholars, I used to spend hours at a time wandering through the streets, and sometimes I wouldn't get home until dawn was breaking.

I was living at that time on Ripon Street—which runs off Wellesley Street, the main thoroughfare—in the southern part of the city, very close to the Indian quarter. I liked to leave home right after supper and wander through those narrow alleys, between walls overrun with flowering bushes, until I left behind the last Anglo-Indian villas and plunged into the labyrinth of the little Indian houses, where the pulsing life never ceases. The uninitiated would think that the Indians in this part of Calcutta never sleep. At any hour of the day you have only to pass by their houses and you will find them on the verandas, or on the edge of the sidewalk, or in their tiny rooms with the doors open to the street, singing, working, chatting, or playing cards. It is the quarter of the poor, and the nighttime din here is so interlaced with music and the sound of the tam-tam that you would think it always a holiday. The acetylene lamps throw a harsh light all around, the scent of the hookah and the sweetish smoke of opium mingle with those other unforgettable odors of the Indian quarters—cinnamon blossoms, damp stables, milk, stale boiled rice, sweets made with honey and fried in deep fat, and hundreds of other nuances impossible to identify in which you sometimes seem to recognize the odor of eucalyptus leaves, or the scent of the blossoms of the "Queen of the Night," which is so like raw incense. You encounter all this as soon as you leave the European quarters or the big parks, where the steaming juices of the jungle are enough to make you dizzy. You encounter all this—and yet in every street you always find a new nuance, sometimes in sharp contrast with the preceding synthesis, from which it stands out for a few moments with surprising boldness.

5

For me, captivated as I was by the magic of the Calcutta nights, eager to enjoy them in as many different ways as possible—for I liked to alternate the boisterous nights of the Indian quarters with nights of complete solitude in the vast park of the Maidan or at the Lakes, where I could forget that I was on the edge of a city with more than a million inhabitants—for me, I say, the nighttime companionship of Bogdanof and Van Manen was a true delight. At first, before I knew the two scholars very well, we used to go for a stroll right after dinner along Ellenborough Course, the great avenue which crosses the Maidan. Before long we set off for the Lakes, from which we would return long after midnight. Van Manen was the most talkative one among us, first of all because he was the oldest, and secondly because he had led a life which was full from all points of view, and he knew India, especially Bengal, like few Europeans. And it was he who one evening invited us for the first time to Serampore, where a friend of his, Budge, had his bungalow. He borrowed an automobile from the Calcutta Club, and we set off without further ado right after nightfall.

Serampore lies some fifteen miles to the north of the city on the right bank of the Hooghly, the river which connects the Ganges with the Gulf of Bengal. On the opposite bank lies Titagarh. Good roads, one starting from Howrah, the other from Chitpur, link Calcutta with the two ancient settlements, a good part of which have now disappeared. Budge, Van Manen's friend, had his bungalow a few miles to the west of Serampore, in an area which was still wooded.

It was an old building, repaired many times, but impossible to keep in good condition in the climate of Bengal and so close to the jungle. The bungalow—as Budge modestly called it—reminded me when I saw it for the first time among its palm trees, of those half-neglected villas in Chandernagore, the glorious

French colony near Calcutta. Its villas from the beginning of the last century, with their iron-work fences and wooden pavilions, seem to be quickly swallowed up by the forest. There is nothing more melancholy than a stroll through Chandernagore right after sunset. Eucalyptus trees grow in the neighborhood, and the gloom of the decaying villas, which you can hardly make out in the darkness against the unyielding walls of vegetation, overwhelms you and drives you almost to distraction. Nowhere are ruins more melancholy than in India, and yet nowhere are they less dismal, for they thrill with a new life, sweeter and more musical, the life of grasses, of lianas, of snakes and glowworms. I liked to wander around Chandernagore, because I found there a history which was dead and gone in the rest of India. The history of the first European colonists, so quaint and so dramatic, of the French pioneers who sailed all the way around Africa and part of the Indian peninsula in order to struggle with the jungle, with malaria, with the intense heat—nowhere was their romance borne in upon me with greater force than at Chandernagore. I rediscovered here the old-fashioned scenery of the glorious pioneer, I resurrected his adventurous life, I imagined his legendary mode of existence—and all of this seemed to me the most vain of vanities, in those nights scented with eucalyptus blossoms and lighted only by stars and glowworms.

Budge had bought the bungalow, it seemed, from an Anglo-Indian planter a few years after the war, and he kept it mostly as a place of refuge and rest when the affairs of Calcutta became too much for him. He was a rather strange man, this Budge, a bachelor, very rich, and a luckless hunter; for among the first things we learned about him from Van Manen was his proverbial ineptitude at hunting.

The first time we visited Serampore he himself was at home. He had arrived only a few hours ahead of us, intending to stay two days. We found him with a fat cigar between his teeth, stretched out on a chaise longue on the veranda, heedless of the mosquitoes swarming around. He seemed tired, and hardly raised himself to greet us. He invited us all to have a whisky on ice to restore our strength. Then while supper was being prepared he stayed to chat with Van Manen on the veranda, while Bogdanof and I set off to explore the surroundings.

"Take care not to wake up the snakes," our host called after us as we were going down the steps.

We must have waked a good many snakes, for we were making quite a bit of noise. We headed for the edge of the forest of palm trees, where we caught a glimpse of water. We were unable to decide what it could be, for the moon had not yet come up and by the light of the stars all we could make out was a sheet of water. As we came closer we discovered a fairly large pond, much of which was covered with lotus. Near where we stood the slender shadow of a coconut palm was reflected in the water. Although we were only a few hundred yards from the bungalow—whose acetylene lamps seemed, from here, to be lost in mist, because of the millions of moths and ephemerids—I felt as though we had suddenly been transported to the shore of an enchanted lake, the silence was so profound and the air so full of mystery.

"Let us hope that the good Lord God will have us in His keeping, now as always," said Bogdanof, as he slowly sat down on the shore of the pond.

I smiled in the darkness, for I knew that he meant it seriously. He never took the name of his Lord God in vain. But, whether because I didn't feel tired or because I was wary—only a few months earlier, just as I was about to jump ashore from a boat, a friend had grabbed my arm and with his walking-stick had killed a little green snake in the dry mud where I was going to put my foot—I preferred not to follow his example, and I contented myself with merely leaning against the coconut palm.

"I have always hoped that I shall never meet the Great Snake here on earth," Bogdanof spoke again, guessing my thought. "*Sarparāja,* I think that's what you call it, isn't it?'"

By "you" Bogdanof meant both students of the Sanskrit language and the entire Hindu population of India.

"Yes, *sarparāja*," I said seriously, in agreement, "and also *sarpapati, sarparishi, sarpeshvara,* and there are many other forms too. But they all refer to the Great Snake, as you say . . ."

"Let us pray to God that we never meet it," Bogdanof interrupted me. "Neither in this venomous land of India, nor in the other place, in Hell."

I lit a cigarette. The two of us remained for a long time without uttering a word. Behind us stretched the forest of palm trees, occasionally stirred by a gentle breeze which we could not feel on our foreheads. When the stiff leaves touched each other, you would have thought for a moment that the forest was made entirely of copper. You would turn your head in surprise, for the metallic ring contrasted strangely with the air saturated with the odors of plant life. And a shiver would run down the length of your spine. Then all would become still again, and silence would settle once more over the forest and the lake. We remained there lost in thought, our gaze turned inwards, as can happen at the sight of a motionless sheet of water, and waited for the lotuses to open.

"It is very beautiful indeed," Bogdanof finally whispered, more to himself than to me. "We must come here again . . ."

9

2.

... AND we did come back, a great many times. We didn't always find Budge there, but Van Manen knew the servants, and we never failed to find a good supper, whisky on ice, cigarettes of every sort—and, whenever we felt too tired to drive back to Calcutta, comfortable beds with netting to protect us from the mosquitoes. Sometimes we went by boat to Titagarh, where there were ponds full of fish and crayfish, and we would stroll along the bank of the river until we were tired. The woods were sparser and more varied on this side of the Hooghly, for this was where the great fields of rice and sugar cane started— but the air was just as perfumed and the night just as full of mystery.

When Budge set out to go hunting in the jungle he never invited us. One evening we happened to arrive unannounced and met him outside the bungalow. He hadn't bagged any-thing, of course, but he was sunburned, dusty, and thirsty.

"Nothing but birds not fit to eat," he said, instead of greeting us, in an attempt, no doubt, to justify his returning empty-handed.

But we had a fine time that night. Van Manen told us about

the days of his friendship with Leadbeater, when the latter was head of the Theosophical Society, while Budge told us of his experiences in Java, where he had commenced his career as an industrialist. We continued to sit around the table until a very late hour, although the light bothered Bogdanof and he was longing to go down to his favorite spot on the shore of the lake. Budge stopped suddenly in the middle of an anecdote—which promised in any case to be long and complicated—and exclaimed:

"You'd never guess whom I met this evening on the edge of the forest, as I was on my way home. Suren Bose!"

We couldn't believe it. What could Bose be doing, at night, in the woods near Serampore? He was a man you wouldn't expect to run into except at the University—for he was a distinguished professor, although the youngest of all his colleagues—or on the way to the temple, at Kalighat. Suren Bose had clung resolutely, almost proudly, to his ancient faith. He was one of the few professors in Calcutta who wasn't ashamed to go around in a *dhoti* and to mark his forehead in saffron with the sign of the Shaivite sect.

"He probably came to visit some relative at Serampore," said Van Manen. "For I find it hard to believe that he took the trouble to come way out here for some love affair . . ."

He began to laugh, but the rest of us were disturbed. It struck us as highly unlikely that the serious-minded Suren Bose would come out to the edge of the forest for a love affair. And Budge assured us that he had no relatives at Serampore; his family was from Orissa, that he knew very well.

"Besides, he pretended not to see me," he added.

Then I recalled that I had once, at the University, heard Suren Bose mentioned in connection with tantric practices. It appeared that Bose belonged to this occult school, concerning which all

11

sorts of legends are current, especially in India. I should explain that I had studied Tantra with great avidity as I found it expounded in its classic texts, but that up until that time I had never had any connection with anyone who practiced its precepts. The tantric initiation involves a number of secret rituals, which no one would dare—or be able—to reveal to you.

"It could be that he came out here in search of some place suitable for tantric practices," I said.

And because no one took my words seriously, I persisted. I knew from my reading that certain tantric meditations and rituals require a doleful setting, a cemetery or a place where the dead are burned. I knew that sometimes the one being initiated in secret rituals must prove his self-mastery by spending an entire night sitting on a corpse in a *çmaçāman* (cremation ground), in the most complete mental concentration. These particulars, and many others equally dreadful, I trotted out for my companions—not so much to account for Suren Bose's presence on the edge of the forest, as because I had let myself be carried away by their baleful fascination, their dreadful magic. Actually, I had almost forgotten about Bose, and was giving a spirited account of these things because I didn't know what to make of them and yet couldn't doubt their authenticity. I was hoping, furthermore, that Van Manen, who had a very fine understanding of Asian occultism, would take part in the discussion, as usual, with his boundless erudition. But this time he contented himself with nodding his head absent-mindedly.

"No one knows exactly what the secret tantric ritual consists of," he said, somewhat annoyed that I had tried to draw him out.

"It can't be anything but a demoniacal orgy," put in Bogdanof, who saw the work of the devil everywhere in Hinduism. "Some poor madmen who seek the salvation of their souls by sitting on corpses and meditating! We all ought to cross ourselves!"

"Actually, I don't see what poor Suren Bose has to do with all these things," Budge reminded us. "Let's get back to the subject . . ."

I realized that I had made a *faux pas* by telling them about cremation grounds and meditations on corpses here near the forest, in the middle of the night—so I lit another cigarette, with a smile of hypocritical penitence. But, to be frank, I was sorry to see that my brief, though impassioned, exposition of tantric practices had been received with such reserve. I was very young at the time, and quite proud of the few things I knew about the Indian soul. I wanted at all costs to show these men who had spent their lives in India that I too knew something about the impenetrable mysteries of Indian religion and magic.

Despite the best efforts of Budge—who continued with the interrupted anecdote—the rest of the night did not have the charm of our usual conversations. As if by tacit agreement, not one of us wanted to go to bed, and no one thought it right to start back to Calcutta before dawn. Instead, we all filled our glasses with whisky—even Bogdanof, who was known for his moderation—and carried on the conversation with a sad apathy until almost three in the morning. Then we got up from the table and went, each of us, to lie down in the rooms prepared for us since the evening before.

3.

Of course we quickly forgot the whole business. When we next set out for Serampore a few evenings later, none of us had any thought of Suren Bose and my *faux pas* in talking about tantrism. I wouldn't have thought any more about it either if one November afternoon—clear and indescribably melodious—I hadn't run into Suren Bose, right after leaving the University grounds. He had always manifested towards me a warm, almost affectionate, feeling, whether because I was the only Rumanian in the entire University, or because I was so diligently studying the religions of his own ancestors. He stopped me to ask how I was getting along with my studies. I replied that my professors were satisfied, but that I myself sometimes wondered whether I would ever really get anywhere with them. He started to smile, and patted me encouragingly on the shoulder. Then I asked him, all of a sudden, whether he had any friends at Serampore, since Budge said that he had caught sight of him not long ago on the outskirts of the town. I was careful not to tell him the real truth: on the edge of the forest.

"I haven't been to Serampore since I was a child," he replied, still smiling. "Old Mr. Budge must have confused me with somebody else."

I looked at him in some perplexity. It would have been difficult to confuse him with anyone else: those firm features, that high forehead, those penetrating eyes—you didn't see them too often in Bengal, where the men found it hard to escape obesity, and everyone had the same round face, the same soft jaw line.

". . . Especially since I wear this garment which is so very common," he added with a little laugh, indicating his *dhoti.*

He looked me straight in the eye and regarded me searchingly.

"Since when are you on such good terms with a millionaire?" he continued, questioning me.

I felt somewhat disconcerted, and, as if to excuse myself, I told him of the excursions that Van Manen, Bogdanof, and I made to Serampore, just now when the nights were so beautiful. He listened to me with great attention, as if every word I said had a special significance for him.

"Oh, those nights at Serampore!" I exclaimed, trying in vain to escape the spell of his gaze.

"Everywhere in Bengal the nights are truly beyond all comparison," he said thoughtfully. "But if Van Manen is always with you, you know he must be drawn to Serampore by something else. Budge's liquor!"

He began to laugh, as if to let me know that he had made a good joke. In fact, nearly everybody joked about Van Manen in this way, for his thirst was well known in all the circles of scholars, snobs, and millionaires in Calcutta—which Van Manen frequented with complete impartiality.

With these words we parted; and when I saw Van Manen at the Library on Park Street, the first thing I told him about was my conversation with Bose. I think I too was gleeful at the idea that Budge had confused some poor Bengali peasant with the great savant Suren Bose, whom he boasted of having known for so many years. Van Manen made great fun of this confusion. He picked up the phone and called Budge at his office. He told him the whole story, adding a few digs of his own, and kept calling him "old Mr. Budge," as Bose had put it so baldly. But Budge was evidently in no mood for joking, for after listening for a few moments Van Manen hung up, smiling.

"He insists that he did see him just the same," he told me. "He stubbornly maintains that he saw him, just as I see you right now. And he also says that he really doesn't much care whether Bose was at Serampore or not. And he doesn't think this is any concern of a librarian at an Asiatic Society."

"Nor of a serious student either," I said, completing his thought, and got up from my chair to go into the reading room.

"I think he's right," Van Manen ended. "I'll tell him so myself, when I see him."

He saw him that very evening, at a club where they sometimes dined, along with a couple of dozen snobs and big industrialists. But I forgot to ask him, the next day, whether they had had any discussion of the case of Suren Bose. The next time the three of us met, a few evenings later, we had many other things to talk about. Van Manen was trying to convince Bogdanof that Buddhism was not a doctrine so easily refuted, and that in any case he, as a scholar, shouldn't allow himself to judge a strange religion like a missionary. They had been carrying on this controversy, at varying intervals, for nearly five years. And Bogdanof always became indignant when he heard the word "missionary."

"We Orthodox Christians have no missionaries," he said defensively. "I don't understand the missionary mentality. That's the business of you Protestants."

And he turned towards me, knowing that I would agree with him. But Van Manen would not give way.

"In the first place, I'm only a Protestant on my father's side," he explained. "On my mother's side I'm a Catholic. And to the best of my knowledge, the Catholics too have missions, some of them going back as much as a thousand years. What do you say, my young friend?" he asked, turning to me.

Of course he was right. But that was not the end of the dispute. Van Manen was planning to write a manual of Buddhism for the general public, and he was trying to find the simplest and most suitable form of presentation in his discussions with Bogdanof. One evening as we were driving out to Serampore he was once again explaining to him, as he had done so many times before, the law of the twelve causes, as he understood it. And then suddenly he stopped speaking and motioned to the chauffeur to slow down. A hundred feet or so ahead of us a Bengali was walking along the edge of the highway very quickly. I don't know why Van Manen was so surprised to see anyone there at that hour. It wasn't yet completely dark, and we were quite close to the town. Perhaps the mere fact that the man was headed towards the forest suddenly reminded him of Suren Bose. And in fact, when the car passed him we all turned our heads and recognized him. He was walking quickly with his head up, and I saw very clearly the three stripes traced in saffron which marked his forehead above the eyebrows. I am not quite sure, but it seemed to me that his gaze met ours for a moment; however, he didn't recognize us. He didn't seem in the least perturbed at this unexpected encounter with three Europeans who knew him. He paid no attention to us, but continued on his way with the same determination.

"So Budge was right after all," said Van Manen as we speeded up again. "This Suren Bose is up to something fishy . . ."

We looked back once more and saw him enter the forest. A

17

few hundred yards further along we too left the main highway and took the road to the left, towards Budge's bungalow. That evening we talked much about this occurrence, just the three of us, as Budge had stayed in Calcutta. As usual, as soon as we arrived we ordered the servants to get supper ready, while we set off for a walk around the pond. It was the next-to-last night before full moon. We walked along as if in a daze, intoxicated by that invisible cloud of odors which enveloped us ever more powerfully the deeper we went into the forest of coconut palms. Whether because of the unexpected encounter with Suren, or because of the charm of the moonlit atmosphere, we were shaken and unsettled. The silence had now become uncanny, and it seemed as though all nature were holding its breath under the spell of the moon. The shaking of a branch made us tremble too, so unnatural did sound and movement seem to us in this extraordinary universal standstill.

"How can you keep from going out of your mind on a night like this," Bogdanof finally whispered. "This beauty is too terrible not to be tainted. Man has no right to experience such a wonder except in paradise. On earth all beauty of this sort is a temptation of the devil. Especially on the soil of India," he added, as if to himself.

But we didn't answer him. We walked along lazily, unthinking, under a spell. Nothing would have surprised us. Everything seemed possible. And when Van Manen stopped us, raising his arm towards the water, we were prepared for any wonder. With cautious steps we approached and saw endless lines of crabs emerge from the lake. They crawled along clumsily, never getting very far from each other, towards the twisted roots of a fallen palm tree.

"They do that every time the moon is approaching full," Bogdanof explained to us later.

4.

A FEW hours later, not long after midnight, we were ready to leave. All during supper Bogdanof had been melancholy, recalling that it would soon be twelve years since he had last set foot on Russian soil, and twenty-two years that he had been living in Asia. Van Manen, on the other hand, suffered not at all from homesickness. He had long since become reconciled to the thought that death would find him here, in India, where he had spent two-thirds of his life. I took no part in this discussion, since I was much younger, and it was scarcely two years since I had come to India.

"You'll see later on," Bogdanof said to me.

Then the conversation turned to completely different topics, and when we got in the car to return to Calcutta, Bogdanof had long since got over his homesickness. In addition it was hard to remain untouched by a night which made you forget every earthly bond, every personal sorrow. Even the chauffeur seemed overcome by so much beauty. Van Manen told him to drive slowly, and we started off.

We drove as usual with the headlights on, although there was a moon. After getting in the car, I lighted a cigarette from

Bogdanof's cigarette-case; he smoked nothing but cigarettes made from Egyptian tobacco, which he ordered especially from Aden. I was lost in thought as I smoked. Van Manen was telling us, as he had done so many times before, how to get along with learned women. From time to time, of course, I had to put in an exclamation or a word of approval—but I did this with growing concern. I couldn't get over the feeling that we had taken the wrong road, that we should have reached the main highway by this time. I wasn't quite sure what was happening, but I didn't seem to recognize the country we were passing through. This feeling that we had lost our way developed in me by stages. At one point I closed my eyes in order to concentrate better, and then opened them again suddenly. I didn't recognize anything around me. We might have been in a completely unknown part of Bengal, so strange did the surroundings look to me.

"But where are we now?" I asked, disturbed.

My companions looked with the same astonishment at the bigger and bigger trees which lined both sides of the road.

"I think we've taken the wrong road," said Bogdanof, alarmed, as though he had only now become aware of the situation.

The chauffeur was driving along with suspicious indifference. Van Manen called to him in Hindustani that we had lost our way.

"We can't possibly get lost," he replied without turning his head. "From Budge Sahib's there isn't any other road . . ."

But his words didn't reassure us. None of us recognized our surroundings, although we knew perfectly well that the chauffeur was right. We had traveled this road at least thirty times, and were all aware that there wasn't any other going out to the highway. We peered in perplexity in all directions, beginning to feel frightened at the solitude, at these unfamiliar trees all around us, with their branches more and more joined together above us, as if they wanted to overcome and overwhelm us.

"Drive faster," Van Manen called again, sounding rather nervous.

The headlights shone more brightly, and we all leaned forward, trying to peer as far ahead as possible, to see if we were approaching the highway. But all we saw was the same unfamiliar road, stretching on endlessly as far as our eyes could see.

"We'd better turn back!" Bogdanof exclaimed suddenly. We had been traveling for half an hour, and we should have reached the highway in five or six minutes.

"Back!" cried Van Manen, frowning.

The chauffeur picked a spot where he could turn the car around, and obeyed the order without a word.

"He's drunk," muttered Van Manen.

But although he had spoken softly, and in English, the chauffeur heard him, for he answered at once, politely, in Hindustani.

"I have never touched liquor in all my life, Director Sahib!"

Bogdanof was becoming more and more impatient, trying to pierce the darkness with his gaze and crossing himself.

"I don't understand what can have happened," he marveled. "If we had gone in the opposite direction, we would have ended up in the forest after a few hundred yards, or would have landed in the pond."

"We'll soon see what's happened," muttered Van Manen.

I tried to tell by the trees about how much farther we had to go to reach the spot where I had definitely noticed for the first time that we were on the wrong road, but I was unable to identify any landmarks. I was about to express my amazement to my companions when we heard, all of us, the dreadful scream of a woman—very close to us. The chauffeur stopped the car suddenly, terrified. We huddled together, dumfounded.

21

"What was that?" I finally asked.

"A woman must have been stabbed," said Van Manen, turning pale.

But we didn't dare get out of the car to try to do anything. I don't know how long we remained thus, petrified with terror. We heard nothing but the sound of the motor, and that seemed to be all that assured us that these things were really happening. Suddenly, a few dozen yards ahead of us, the same woman's scream pierced the air again—followed by a heart-rending cry for help.

"Ma'lum! Gelum! Banchao! Rokkhe koro!"

I understood Bengali well enough to grasp the sense of the words: "I'm dying! I'm finished! Help! Help me!"

We all jumped out of the car, except the chauffeur, and although we couldn't make out a thing in the direction from which the cries had come, we set off at a run towards the sounds. As we were running we heard the screams several times more, and I thought I could make out another couple of words: "Babago! babago!" ("Father! father!")

But we had run in vain. Nowhere did we catch sight of another human being or a single trace of struggle. Van Manen, who was heavier than Bogdanof and I, was puffing along behind us. Bogdanof, with jaws clenched and brows knit, was peering intently into the darkness. We took a closer look at our surroundings. The trees now covered us completely with their thick shade, and we could no longer see a thing. The light of the moon scarcely penetrated here—it merely trembled high up in the vines overhead. Van Manen thought he saw something moving ahead of us, so he stopped and began to call:

"Bepar ki?" ("What has happened?")

Standing still we all listened. There was no answer from any direction. The forest seemed to have turned to stone. Not even the carpet of dead leaves seemed to stir under our feet.

"Bepar ki?" Van Manen called once again.

Then we continued our search, taking good care not to go too far from the road. I don't know how long we wandered there under the trees, expecting at any instant to come upon some horrible scene. I felt weary, and my mind was wandering; I had the continual impression that I was dreaming, and that I couldn't wake up from my dream.

"Let's go back," said Bogdanof, putting his hand to his forehead. "I'm beginning to believe that we've all been subject to an hallucination . . ."

I could have answered him that four people could scarcely have heard the same dreadful scream and the same words, exactly the same words, if we had all been victims of an hallucination. But I felt that he was right—and we returned to the road.

"We've been wandering around in the forest a long time," I said, not seeing the car. "Which way do we go now?"

The other two looked at me in some perplexity.

"Whatever direction we may have gone," said Van Manen uneasily, "the car must be somewhere near at hand. Call that blockhead, won't you?"

I began to yell for all I was worth, and even I myself shivered at the sound of that long drawn out hullabaloo in the solitude of the night. Then we waited in the middle of the road, peering in puzzlement in all directions.

"Maybe he went to look for us," I said.

"But where's the car?" asked Bogdanof through clenched jaws. "Surely he wouldn't go off and leave us here, in the middle of the jungle . . ."

"He can't have left," Van Manen reassured us quickly. "We

would have heard the motor, since we never got very far from the road . . . He's fallen asleep in the car, that's what it must be."

We set off in the direction where we knew we had left the car. The moon was now shining full on us, for the road was becoming wider and wider.

"He's gone off, no doubt about it!" whispered Bogdanof again. "He deserves to be shot . . ."

Van Manen couldn't bring himself to believe any such thing. He kept mopping his brow and cheeks with his handkerchief.

"In any case, we must do something," he said very slowly.

"Let's walk back to Budge's," Bogdanof decided. "We ought to reach there by morning, anyway . . ."

At that instant we thought we glimpsed, not far ahead of us on the right side of the road, a lantern moving off with a swinging motion into the heart of the forest. We looked at each other, not daring to breathe. It struck us as very strange to catch sight of a man with a lighted lantern at that hour of the night and in such a place. Especially after all that had happened to us. And yet every one of us felt a certain sinister attraction towards that little light, which was rapidly disappearing into the jungle. When Bogdanof motioned us to follow him, neither Van Manen nor I demurred. We forgot that not long before the blood had frozen in our veins at hearing a woman's scream and her cries for help. The light was, at least, a sign of life. It was being carried by someone who was no doubt headed towards a house or towards the highway that we too were looking for.

We set off as fast as we could to overtake him.

5.

MAKING our way into the forest, we lost track of him after a few minutes. The three of us were walking along close to each other, I in front—as the youngest—with Van Manen right behind me. We pushed on fearlessly, with a strange assurance that I cannot account for, under the trees that would have frightened us only an hour before. The jungle, so terrifying to every white man, especially in the middle of the night, seemed to us robbed of all menace. We weren't thinking of snakes or of startled animals— and we no longer felt that fear which seizes you in India as soon as you find yourself alone deep in the forest.

"I can't see anything any more," said Van Manen, with a note of tragic resignation in his voice.

We didn't answer him, either one of us. We continued to push ahead, almost without being aware of what we were doing; we felt that we couldn't stop right there in the middle of the forest, that we had to keep moving along, however absurd our decision might seem.

"He must have taken a path which we have missed," said Bogdanof.

"He must have known the way, at least," I added, "since he disappeared so quickly . . ."

The further we went, the more inextricably we seemed to be getting entangled in the forest; thick vines began to brush the top of our heads, and our feet sank deeper and deeper into the layer of dead leaves, ferns, and moss. But a blind stubbornness impelled us on in the same direction. None of us felt any desire to turn back or to try to find a different way through. We kept on, despite all obstacles, pushing ahead with difficulty, almost cutting our way through the endless thicket ahead.

"I think I see the light again," Bogdanof suddenly exclaimed.

We stopped to take a look, scarcely daring to breathe. This time, very close to us, a dim light could be seen which certainly could not be the rushlight we had set out to follow some time earlier. We headed towards it, summoning up our last reserves of strength. We had been walking only a few minutes when we found that we were approaching the edge of the forest and saw that the light we had glimpsed was a reflection from the embers in a charcoal kiln. Before we reached it, however, we saw that there were a number of kilns with glowing embers, and that not very far from us, on our left, rose a very strange building surrounded by a grey stone wall.

"We must be approaching Serampore from the other side, from the north," said Van Manen. "But how on earth did we ever get here?"

It seemed very strange to us not to meet anyone at the charcoal kilns. It is true that in most of them the fire was nearly out; still, we didn't catch sight of a single soul anywhere. We were too tired, however, to do much looking around, so we headed straight for the house.

"Whoever lives here, Hindu or Moslem, he'll have to take us in," said Van Manen.

He had taken the lead, partly because he spoke Bengali better than we did, partly because his name was well known all over Bengal, or at least the name of the Asiatic Society of which he was the librarian. When we reached the gate, an old man came out to meet us. He didn't seem particularly surprised to see us, at that hour of the night, outside this house hidden so deep in the jungle.

"Who is your master?" Van Manen asked him.

The old man stood there without stirring for a few moments, as if he hadn't heard what was said. Van Manen asked him once more, almost shouting. As if he were waking up from a long sleep, the old man whispered, "Nīlāmvara Dāsa . . ."

"I think I've heard that name," said Bogdanof.

"It sounds rather old-fashioned," was Van Manen's opinion. "I've never heard it in Calcutta."

Then, turning to the old man, he said, "Go wake your master and tell him that Van Manen Sahib and two other sahibs have had an accident and ask him to take us in for the night."

He had to repeat his words three times before the old man showed any sign of leaving.

"He must be completely deaf," observed Bogdanof.

But despite all that was happening, I had a strange feeling that my dream was continuing and that I hadn't yet succeeded in waking up. Those abandoned kilns, this odd-looking house surrounded on three sides by woods, the old man who didn't seem to understand what was said to him, in whatever dialect Van Manen addressed him—all this disturbed me and made me anxious. I have no idea how long it was before the old man returned, with a lantern in his hand. Time seemed to have stopped, and I felt I was living only fragmentarily, in separate episodes only.

"My master invites you in," said the old man.

Perhaps he spoke too softly, perhaps I was too tired or didn't yet understand Bengali well enough, but I grasped the sense of his words more by guessing than by actual understanding.

"How strangely he speaks," I said to Van Manen.

"He has a rustic accent," he replied. "Until you get used to it . . ."

The house looked quite old, a rarity in this part of Bengal, where the Moslem invaders had been particularly ruthless all through the eighteenth century. We went into an inner court-yard, half-paved, with a number of *ficus religiosa,* that sacred bush so venerated by the Hindus, growing in the corners. From here we had a good view of the nearest rooms, which were very large, with latticed windows; these were no doubt the men's quarters. I got the impression that we were expected; several torches had been lighted, in addition to many oil lamps and rushlights, whose timid gleam we could make out particularly on the stairs leading to the women's quarters. We were invited into a room with a flagstone floor made of red gritstone, where we were met by a middle-aged man with a very pale face and staring eyes—and he spoke to us right from the start in Bengali.

"Please wait here for a few moments, until they have prepared the rooms for your night's rest," he said.

I had considerable trouble understanding him, for he too spoke a very strange sort of Bengali, such as I had until then met only in books. Ordinarily an educated Bengali or one of any social standing greets European guests in English. Except in special cases he would consider it an insult to address a stranger in Bengali; that would mean that he considered him a poor peasant or a servant. So much the more strange, then, did our host's reception seem to me. Van Manen, however, who had a perfect command of Bengali, didn't let himself be intimidated by this behavior—and he asked permission to sit down in an easy chair, continuing at the same time to make our excuses for this intrusion at such an hour. Nīlāmvara seemed lost in his own thoughts as he listened, and after Van Manen had finished making excuses, Nīlāmvara still remained standing, looking at each of us in turn, as if he couldn't bring himself to believe that we were really there before him. For a long time he didn't utter a single word, and this silence disturbed and unnerved us almost to the point of panic.

"A stupid accident has occurred," said Bogdanof in English, no longer able to stand his icy stare.

But our host didn't even seem to hear. He continued to look at us, occasionally shuddering over his whole body. Bogdanof moved a step closer and repeated what he had said in a louder voice. Our host tried to smile, and answered him, although in a whisper: "Ami imreji bujhte pārchi na." ("I don't understand English.")

This admission struck me as very strange indeed. Even schoolboys understood English; was it possible that Nīlāmvara had not attended a modern school, but had received only an orthodox education, such as can be acquired in a *thol?* But his manner of speaking struck me as equally strange; he pronounced the words completely differently from the way I was used to hearing them, and he uttered them with a difficulty whose nature I could not determine. He brought out each word only with considerable effort, and yet we could see no reason why this should be so.

"The rooms for the night's rest will soon be ready for Your Highnesses," he added after a long pause, smiling as if in a dream.

This time he looked attentively at Van Manen. He too had begun to be perplexed at Nīlāmvara's archaic way of speaking, and perhaps also at his wild glances. Now that we could see him better, Nīlāmvara really did impress us as strange-looking. The difficulty with which he moved, those unaccountable shudders

29

that shook his body at intervals, as though he were taken with a chill, the unnatural glassy stare, the fists which he kept clenched the whole time—all these things now began to draw our attention. His way of looking at us was utterly strange. Sometimes I got the impression that he was animated by an invisible force, and that if it were withdrawn he would stand there before us stiff and lifeless, with just the trace of a smile.

And then, we couldn't understand what was going on in this house, so brightly illuminated, and yet, as far as our ears could tell, deserted. Such an event—the arrival of three strangers in the middle of the night—would never pass unnoticed in an Indian household. We expected to see shadows moving around us, to catch sight of feminine silhouettes peeking at us from the corners or from behind the gratings, to hear those stifled whispers of servants wakened from sleep, their soft steps on the flagstones of the courtyard.

"The rooms for the night's rest will soon be ready . . ." Nīlāmvara said, beginning the same sentence for the third time.

Nevertheless, no one came to announce that our rooms were ready. We would have liked to withdraw, not because we were tired—after all that had happened we were too worked up even to think of sleep—but in order to escape from the unnerving presence of our host. Suddenly, Van Manen looked at us and spoke to us in English.

"We've completely forgotten to ask him about the woman whose screams we heard on the road . . ."

And in fact, that was the one thing he hadn't mentioned. Van Manen had told him we had had an accident, making up a story that our car had broken down and that the chauffeur had stayed behind to guard it, but he hadn't said a thing about the cries for help we had heard an hour earlier. None of us could understand how we could have spent so much time with this man—

30

who certainly ought to know something about it—without asking him about it, without telling him the truth. The recollection of the cries in the forest now upset us all over again. I had the feeling that I had suddenly waked from the sleep into which I had fallen as soon as we started to follow that little light—and once again I felt afraid. I would have liked to do something, even now, even after having lost so much precious time. That poor woman might have given up the ghost, while we were wandering through a good part of the jungle to ask for hospitality at the house of Nīlāmvara Dāsa. What accursed spell had robbed us all of our wits, and detained us there for such a long time with a man who kept repeating the same words every ten minutes? . . .

"Tell him; perhaps he knows what it's all about," Bogdanof suggested to Van Manen.

Just as he was, lying back in the wooden easy chair, Van Manen began to narrate what had happened, hardly able to control his agitation. But at his very first words our host covered his face with his hands and groaned. We all went closer to him.

"Lila, Lila!" he groaned.

Then he stammered a few words which were meaningless to me.

"What is he saying? what is he saying?" we asked Van Manen eagerly.

"I can't understand him either," he replied.

Then he asked once again in Bengali, "What has happened? Who was it?"

The same groans and the same unintelligible words, in which we could make out only the name of Lila, were accompanied now by a cry of grief.

"I think it was his daughter," Van Manen explained to us.

31

"But I can't understand what he's trying to say; he's talking so fast . . ."

"They must have killed her," whispered Bogdanof. "But how did he hear about it? And if he knew it, why hasn't he said anything before this?"

But Van Manen didn't dare ask him anything more. We remained speechless, uncertain whether we should withdraw without telling him, or whether we should wait for the return of the old man who had been getting the rooms ready for us for such a long time.

"But why on earth couldn't anyone come to her aid?" exclaimed Van Manen suddenly. "She can't have been all alone; the women here never go out alone, especially not in the middle of the night . . ."

At that moment the old man came into the room and approached us with weary steps.

"There she is! They're bringing her; she's over there," he said to us very slowly, motioning with his arm.

We all rushed to the door. I got the impression that the courtyard was full of shadows, and that several strangely dressed men in turbans were carrying a bier made of branches. But I couldn't make out anything very clearly. And I didn't hear anything, no wailing, no cries. I turned around startled with a feeling that someone had passed close by me. I caught sight of Nīlāmvara moving away with difficulty, as if every step he took called for all the strength he could muster.

"We can't stay here," whispered Bogdanof. "You can't ask hospitality of a man whose daughter or wife has been murdered . . ."

"Yes, it's better that we leave," said Van Manen.

We would have liked to let somebody know we were leaving, and to apologize once more to our host, but there was no longer

32

anyone in the courtyard. The old man too had disappeared, as if the earth had swallowed him up. Bogdanof was the first to head for the gate, and he didn't even dare look back. It was with a sense of relief that we saw again the half-extinguished fires in the charcoal kilns which we had first seen in the clearing in front of the house.

6.

It was only some time later that weariness overcame me, after we had left the house and were skirting the edge of the forest. At first it was like a slight dizziness, then exhaustion gradually came over me, and I could scarcely find the strength to lean against the trunk of a tree, in order not to topple over on the ground unconscious.

I couldn't understand what was happening to me. I wasn't aware whether I was alone or whether my two companions were waiting for me to come to my senses again. I don't know how long I remained like that, leaning on the trunk—but when I awoke, day had begun to dawn. I still felt exhausted and my mind was in a daze; I had no exact recollection of all that had happened.

To my surprise I soon discovered my two companions sitting on the grass a few yards away from the spot where I had stopped. Van Manen seemed to be asleep, with his head resting in his hands; Bogdanof was half stretched out on the ground. Not without difficulty, I went up to them.

"What has happened?" I asked, with an attempt at a smile. "Why on earth did we stop here?"

They too appeared worried as they looked at me, and I was shocked at the dark circles under Bogdanof's eyes, his pale forehead, and the way he kept staring at me uncomprehendingly.

"I think all three of us must have succumbed to fatigue," he said finally.

I went to sit down next to them, dragging my feet along with difficulty. I might have been sick in bed for weeks on end, I felt so weak. My eyesight became blurred at the slightest effort. I was nevertheless aware that day had dawned and that the grass was wet with dew. For some time longer we remained like that, without uttering a word. But my companions, and especially Van Manen, appeared to be so exhausted that I felt obliged to do something. I got up, with difficulty, and started to peer all around me as attentively as I was capable of doing. The locality didn't look so unfamiliar to me. The forest was sparse in these parts, just a few ancient palm trees, tall locust trees, and sweet smelling bushes.

I began to walk on, very cautiously, and I hadn't gone more than ten steps when I discovered, very close to us, the road which ran off the main highway in the direction of Budge's bungalow. This discovery gave me strength. Turning towards my companions I called, "We're not far from the bungalow!"

They must have been dumbfounded at this news, for we had imagined that we were somewhere to the north of Serampore. I saw Bogdanof get up, with difficulty, and stretch out a hand to Van Manen. I wanted to run to help them, but at the very first step I felt the ground whirl around under me. I had to stop until I recovered again. My two companions soon reached me. Van Manen's cheeks were sunken, his eyelids were dark, and his glance was that of a man who doesn't understand what is happening to him. He was breathing heavily, and he kept his mouth open. Bogdanof's hands were shaking continually. He

35

looked around in all directions, unable to bring himself to believe that we were really close to Budge's bungalow.

"We must have been wandering around all night long," I said, in order to give them courage. "The chauffeur must be on the other side of the forest waiting for us."

When he heard the chauffeur mentioned, blood rushed to Van Manen's cheeks. He couldn't keep back a terrible curse, such as I had never believed him capable of uttering. But at least this curse revived us a little. We stepped out on the road and set off, slowly, for the bungalow.

"I still don't understand too well what happened to us," Van Manen said finally. "Such a strange fatigue . . ."

Before long the sun came up. Its strong light woke us completely, and we started walking faster. In any case we had only about half an hour's walk to the bungalow. What was our surprise to find our car waiting for us in front of the veranda! The chauffeur was dozing. A few servants were toiling in the yard; they were amazed when they saw us come in, haggard with fatigue, our clothes torn, our shoes dusty. Van Manen went straight over to the chauffeur and began hitting him, cursing him at the same time. Stupefied, the poor fellow made no move to defend himself. He only raised his arm to cover his eyes and groaned.

"Why did you run away, you beast?" yelled Van Manen. "Suppose we had got lost in the jungle and left our bones there?"

The servants had all gathered around the car, flabbergasted. They could hardly believe that Van Manen, who was well known for his kind heart and his good nature, was actually striking and cursing someone.

"We survived, but only by a miracle," said Bogdanof in Hindustani, so that the servants might understand it, and might

36

understand Van Manen's anger. "This jackass left us on the road and ran away, came back home . . ."

"We wandered around all night long," I added.

Everybody looked at us in astonishment. Those who had come up later glanced from the chauffeur to us, with no idea of what was happening.

"But he waited for you all night right here," the bungalow watchman finally made bold to say.

At this the others too plucked up their courage. "He was here! He never stirred from here!"

At first we didn't quite understand what they meant. We interpreted it to mean that the chauffeur, seeing that we didn't emerge from the forest again, had returned to the bungalow and waited for us in front of the veranda until morning. That, however, was precisely what Van Manen was accusing him of: having lost patience so quickly, there on the road, and having gone back to the bungalow.

"But he never left here!" the watchman insisted. "I was talking with him until quite late, and he never stirred from here."

"I was surprised that Director Sahib hadn't yet started back to Calcutta!" exclaimed the chauffeur.

At this point I felt the blood rush to my cheeks. All these people must have believed that we had had too much to drink and could no longer remember what we had done.

"What do you mean?" said Bogdanof. "How can you say you never stirred from here? Didn't we start off, all of us, at one in the morning, and then didn't we lose our way, and didn't we hear a woman scream in the forest . . ."

The chauffeur hesitated and dumbly looked around the circle in search of aid. He didn't dare to defend himself by telling the truth. But when Van Manen began to shout and to remind him of everything we had said when we realized that we had lost our way, the fellow decided to speak.

"We never left at all, Director Sahib! The car never moved from the yard . . ."

"That's the truth, that's how it was," said the others, backing him up.

Van Manen lost his temper again. "In other words, you're making us out to be liars!"

"Perhaps you took another car," said the chauffeur, in an attempt to find some other explanation. "And just look, the car is still just as clean as when I washed it last night . . ."

Van Manen turned to us. "He's crazy! They've all gone out of their minds here! Come on, let's go in the house . . ."

We found it open, which it should not have been, for as soon as we left the watchman was supposed to lock all the rooms.

"He's putting on an act, with the aid of the watchman and the servants," said Bogdanof as soon as we were alone. "They must have thought we were all drunk . . ."

"He'll pay for this dearly, I'll see to that," muttered Van Manen, taking off his coat and dropping into a wicker chair.

I felt obliged to put my oar in too. For I thought I had caught a sarcastic look in the eyes of some of the servants when I told them that we had spent the night wandering around in the jungle. I was infuriated at the thought that they had considered us to be so drunk that they presumed to make fun of us.

"For one thing, I'm suspicious of his alibi about the clean car, which he claims is just as it was last night," I said. "That little detail lets the cat out of the bag: the whole story was cooked up right from the beginning . . ."

The coolness of the house and the fatigue we had been

fighting off with such difficulty for the last few hours induced us to break off this discussion; and after washing we all stretched out on the beds we usually slept in, and before long we were all sound asleep.

7.

WE were awakened by Budge, who arrived in the early afternoon to spend a few hours hunting before the sun went down. He didn't seem exactly pleased to find us there. When he came out to go hunting for a short time, he didn't like to run into any of his friends. And he was surprised to find us so tired.

"It seems you all lost your heads last night," he said, speaking to Van Manen in particular.

Once again I felt my cheeks burning. I detected the same embarrassment in Bogdanof.

"Your chauffeur is a criminal," Van Manen began heatedly. And he was about to tell him everything that had happened. But at his very first words, Budge could scarcely keep back a smile any longer.

"The chauffeur says you never even left here," he interrupted him. "And that's what the others say too; furthermore . . ."

"They must all be in cahoots," Bogdanof put in grimly. "Just wait and hear what happened in the end."

Van Manen, irritated, continued with his narration. From time to time we supplied additional details, and the preciseness of our recollections was beginning to make Budge less sure of his ground.

"But I can't understand how you could have lost your way," he interrupted Van Manen again. "There just isn't any other road. You don't have to take my word for it—you can see for yourselves."

"My dear friend," Van Manen said emphatically, "we're telling you how things happened. We'll have to try and find an explanation afterwards."

And again he took up the thread of the story, at the point where, seeing that we still hadn't reached the highway, he had called to the chauffeur to turn back.

"Can you recall anything of what you saw to the left and the right of the road?" asked Budge.

I explained to him what kind of trees I had seen, and how tall they looked to me. Budge got up from his chair.

"My dear friends, forgive me, but nowhere in this district are there any trees like that. Except for the forest of palm trees which you see there"—he waved his arm towards the pond— "there is nothing in this entire region but eucalyptus, coconut palms, and locust trees. This *Urwald* you are telling me about doesn't exist anywhere around here . . ."

"Yet the fact remains that we did *not* dream it all," Bogdanof countered.

"But why can't you wait until you've heard the whole story?" asked Van Manen.

Budge shrugged his shoulders and sat down in the chair again. Van Manen went on with his tale. When he came to the episode of the scream which had so frightened us all, Budge started to smile. But as Van Manen continued his narrative, he began to show signs of impatience. Every time he started to interrupt, however, we stopped him and begged him to listen

41

right to the end. But he had a hard time restraining himself. He kept jumping up from his chair at every new detail we mentioned.

"You're making fun of me!" he finally burst out, when Van Manen described the house of Nīlāmvara Dāsa. "There's no such thing as a house hidden in the jungle anywhere around here. And that's a name I've never heard before. This is a hoax!"

He began to walk around the room, trying to show us by peals of laughter that he was made of tougher stuff and that he was not to be taken in by any hoax. But we didn't feel in the least like laughing. For one thing, we were bothered by the things Budge had told us—things that we too knew very well, of course: that no such house existed, and so forth—and for another, we were exasperated at his incredulity, his ridiculous idea that we were trying to play a joke on him.

"I give you my word of honor that I'll never speak to you again if ever I admit that *this* was a joke," Van Manen proclaimed solemnly. "If you want, take each of us aside separately and ask us the same questions. You will soon be convinced that we all *saw* the same thing. It's difficult to devise a hoax in such a way that it won't be revealed as soon as you begin to check on the details. And there can't be any question of hallucination either, because *I* sat in a chair in Nīlāmvara's house, and these chaps saw me sitting in the chair, and with their own ears they heard me tell him what I've been telling *you* just now."

"And I'm sure he didn't believe you either," said Budge, still trying to make a joke out of the whole thing.

"On the contrary," Van Manen replied cuttingly. "He too knew about the murder of that woman, and he began to groan and cover his face . . ."

Bogdanof and I hastened to confirm this too, adding that we didn't understand what he had said, but could only make out the

42

name of Lila. Budge looked at us with a frown, and this time made no comment. He merely motioned to Van Manen to continue. And for the first time Van Manen was able to tell his tale interrupted only when we put in our comments on this or that detail. When he had finished and was starting to explain how we woke up exhausted at the edge of the forest, and how we discovered that we were quite close to the bungalow, Budge solemnly rose from his chair, and after a pause, during which he seemed to be weighing his words carefully, proceeded to speak with a certain pomposity.

"I give you my word of honor that as long as I have been living in India, I have never heard of any such happening as this. I too have heard tales of all sorts of mysterious and preposterous happenings, but this beats them all. For you see I know Serampore as well as I do Calcutta, and I've hunted for fifty miles all around—and never have I come across any trace of such a house as you describe. So that you may convince yourselves that what I am saying is true, why don't you get dressed and we'll take the car and search the neighborhood. We have three or four hours yet before it gets dark . . ."

Van Manen, Bogdanof, and I looked at each other with some uneasiness. What if we really had been the victims of an illusion? But we had such an exact recollection of our adventure, and we knew how peaceful it had been the night before—and not one of us had drunk more whisky than he should have. We simply couldn't doubt that we really had talked with Nīlāmvara Dāsa. Van Manen jumped out of bed with an air of decision.

"Let's go!" he said to us. "But let's go in your car," he added, turning to Budge. "For I'll tear that jackass of a chauffeur limb from limb if I ever set eyes on him again. He claims that he never even stirred from here!"

"That's what puzzles me most of all," said Budge. "For even

43

supposing that you were quite drunk—a thing, I hasten to add, which I do not for one instant believe—I don't understand how you could have got into the jungle without the chauffeur or one of the other servants seeing you. They assure me that they hadn't gone to bed, that they were waiting for your orders."

"Then why on earth didn't they notice that the rooms were empty?" asked Van Manen. "Who put out the lamps? Didn't anyone come in until morning to bring tea or to see if we needed anything?"

Budge remained lost in thought. Van Manen's questions had shaken his certainty. The chauffeur and the servants must undoubtedly know something very strange, if they were trying to conceal it with such resourcefulness.

"I'll question them later," he said. "Meanwhile, let's satisfy ourselves that neither the road, the house, nor the people you met last night exist."

We began to dress in haste. When I looked in the mirror I was shocked to see how pale my face was and what heavy circles I had under my eyes. My whole face was ravaged as if from a terrible illness. When we went down to the car we found the whole yard full of people. All the servants, as well as some peasants on their way to Serampore, had gathered to see us. I felt I must find something or other to say until we were all settled in Budge's car, so I turned to Van Manen.

"You didn't tell him that we saw Suren Bose again last night, right on the edge of the forest."

This information seemed to have a remarkable effect on Budge. His eyes seemed to bore through us, as though he were angry with us for not telling him about this encounter sooner.

"Perhaps things may not be quite so simple after all," said Budge in a whisper, as if he were speaking to himself.

44

We asked him what he meant, but all he did was mumble to himself while the car was starting up, without saying a single word more. He seemed preoccupied with a thought which he was not ready to disclose to us.

8.

A few moments later I asked Bogdanof for one of his cigarettes which he got on special order from Aden. As I was taking the first puff, I recalled with almost painful exactitude the cigarette I had lighted the evening before, not long after we had started off. I pointed this out to Budge, but he only nodded and said nothing. At that instant the thought flashed through my mind that by estimating how long I had been smoking the cigarette the night before, I could determine fairly closely when I first noticed that we had lost our way. Van Manen kept looking back all the time. He was wondering whether somehow or other we might not have started off in the opposite direction. But he was obliged to recognize what he had been told so many times: that the automobile road ended at the bungalow, and that what seemed to be a continuation of it was only a cart track which soon came to an end at the pond.

This time the car was moving quite slowly. We recognized the scenery we had so often driven past—so different from the forest of the night before. The forest we saw now was some distance away, running along the main highway which came from Calcutta; there, at a spot easy to identify, we had caught sight of

Suren Bose. But along the road leading to the bungalow the forest appears to have been largely cleared away; here there were only isolated trees of several varieties.

We kept looking to the right and to the left until we reached the highway—and I hadn't yet finished smoking my cigarette. I admitted to my companions that I was completely bewildered. Budge ordered the chauffeur to turn back, and this time we drove even more slowly.

"Do you remember the spot where you woke up this morning?" Van Manen asked me.

With some hesitation, I was able to locate it a few minutes later. It was some five hundred yards off the road to the bungalow, in the direction of the forest. We all got out of the car, and I took them over to it. As I came closer, I recognized the tree I had leaned against unconscious.

"Here's where I found the two of you," I said to Van Manen and Bogdanof. "And I think we came from that direction," I added, pointing towards the forest.

"In that case it's very simple," Budge reflected. "We have only to find the tracks you left . . ."

And in fact, a practiced eye could make out, here and there on the carpet of dead leaves, the clumsy impression of the foot of a European. Budge's chauffeur, who seemed to be taking a special interest in this investigation, began following the tracks. He followed them without difficulty for about fifty yards, but then the tracks seemed to leave the woods and lead to a clearing, where they disappeared. We were completely baffled. We couldn't remember crossing any open field, except for the one in front of Nīlāmvara's house, which was surrounded on the other three sides by woods.

"There's nothing left for us to do but search the woods," said Budge. "I know them quite well, I've crossed them in all directions, and I assure you that you won't find any trace of a house anywhere in them. But watch out for snakes."

"But last night we wandered all around in the heart of the jungle and nothing happened to us," said Van Manen.

"In the woods where you were wandering last night the snakes have long since ceased to bite," replied Budge mysteriously.

We continued our search for perhaps half an hour without coming across so much as a shack. Van Manen was beginning to get tired.

"We can go on if you wish," said Budge. "But let me say again that the forest stretches on just as you see it now for several leagues farther."

"There's no point in wearing ourselves out any longer," said Bogdanof. "I feel that this isn't last night's forest."

"There isn't any other," Budge interjected.

We turned back disappointed. Van Manen was peering distractedly in all directions, unable to bring himself to believe it.

"What if last night, without realizing it, we got to the north of Serampore?" he asked.

Budge began walking faster and called back over his shoulder:

"Let's go to Serampore!"

With the car it took us only about ten minutes to get there. But we at once realized that no matter how we had gone, we couldn't get beyond Serampore without running into the main highway coming from Calcutta. There was no way of getting there across country.

"Let's stop at Chatterji's," said Budge. "Perhaps he can enlighten us."

Budge, who knew everybody, had a friend in Serampore too, this Chatterji, a jute merchant. He lived on the edge of town. We found him at home.

48

"I'll ask him about the house and the people as if you just happened to hear about them," Budge explained to us. "Otherwise Chatterji might think you had a bad dream and are trying to have a good laugh at his expense . . ."

If anybody should know all about Serampore, it was Chatterji. But he hadn't heard of any such house in the middle of the jungle either. However, when Van Manen told him about Nīlāmvara Dāsa and his daughter or wife Lila, who had been mysteriously murdered one night, he stared at us in amazement.

"Who told you these things?" he asked, visibly agitated.

"A friend of mine claims he had a talk with him the very night his daughter was killed," Van Manen prevaricated.

"But these things happened some hundred and fifty years ago!" exclaimed Chatterji. "Nīlāmvara Dāsa was one of the most renowned vaishnavas in all Bengal, and his young wife Lila actually was killed by the leader of a Moslem band, who had fallen in love with her and wanted to abduct her. These are things which have long since become legend."

"Do you by any chance know where this Dāsa lived?" asked Budge.

"His house was destroyed, along with the houses of all the other Hindus, in the year 1810," Chatterji told us. "But it can't have been very far from Serampore. He was a very rich man, by the way, and had several houses. His wife was abducted while returning, without sufficient escort, from the city to their summer home. One of her companions, they say, got away and broke the news—but when Dāsa took up the pursuit and was closing in, the robber killed her."

We were too amazed to say anything, and merely looked at each other. Budge persisted with his questions and asked him whether there was anyone named Nīlāmvara Dāsa now living anywhere in the vicinity.

"I don't think there's anyone with just that name," Chatterji replied. "It was a noble family which became extinct at the beginning of the last century. Anyway, no one is named Dāsa any more these days; the modern form of the name is Das."

He fell silent, and seemed surprised at the frightened bewilderment which had seized us all. He let his gaze roam from one of us to the other, not daring to ask, and yet not understanding, why we were so concerned.

"Your friend must have heard about Nīlāmvara from the stories about him which are current around here," said Chatterji at last. "For, as I told you, his memory is still alive, although enveloped in legend. There's no end of ballads which deal with Lila's abduction and murder . . ."

Van Manen suddenly got up from his chair and turned to Budge.

"Let's go!" he said. "I'm simply dead with fatigue . . ."

We said goodnight to Chatterji and started off right for Calcutta. All three of us did, as a matter of fact, feel very tired. For some time no one spoke. Then Van Manen turned to Budge and said:

"I'm sure you understand that there are good reasons why no one must be told of what has happened."

Budge nodded thoughtfully.

"We have, as they say, been subject to a diabolical hallucination," whispered Bogdanof.

"If only it had been a hallucination," Budge interrupted him.

For a while we were all plunged in our own thoughts, and no one said anything.

"I can't understand why Suren Bose felt it necessary to make us witnesses of such a horrible thing," Van Manen said then. "It's going to be awfully difficult now for me ever to shake hands with him again . . ."

50

"Perhaps, without meaning to, *we* interfered with *him*," I said, voicing a thought that had crossed my mind.

"In any case," Van Manen said to me, "what has happened must remain our secret from now on. If you should run into Bose, and can't get away from him, act as if nothing had happened . . ."

9.

NONE of us ever went back to Serampore. Bogdanof was laid low with fever for some time and Van Manen became prey to melancholia, while Budge no longer spent his weekends at his bungalow. As a matter of fact, I found out some months later that he had sold it, for a ridiculous price.

Circumstances which have nothing to do with the present story obliged me to leave Calcutta unexpectedly and to seek quiet in a monastery in the western Himalayas, in the vicinity of Hardwar. I met Suren Bose only once after our adventure at Serampore. I turned pale on seeing him, but I couldn't avoid him. We had a very ordinary conversation, he asking me, as usual, about my studies, and I answering him in a perfunctory way. However, he couldn't resist the temptation to let fly an arrow at Van Manen.

"Our old friend drinks too much for the climate of Bengal," he said. This was an uncalled-for aspersion, since he knew the reason perfectly well.

I didn't know what to say to this, for I had promised not to tell anyone—and least of all Suren Bose—of our adventure at Serampore.

But many months after I had got settled in the Himalayas, at

Rishi Kesh, I nevertheless broke my word and narrated the extraordinary experience to Swami Shivananda, the one man in the whole monastery with whom I had a real meeting of minds. As a matter of fact, I would have found it very difficult not to tell him about it, for he himself had studied and practiced Tantra many years earlier, and I hoped to get from him the solution to so many mysteries which I lacked the experience to comprehend. This Swami Shivananda was, moreover, a most remarkable man in every respect. He had been a doctor in Singapore, he had been married and he had two children—and one fine day he left everything and set off to seek salvation, as he put it, in a monastery in the Himalayas. Some day, perhaps, I shall write the truly amazing life of this ascetic doctor, who had traveled all over India on foot, had taken part in all the religious ceremonies of all the sects and had studied all their philosophies, in search of peace for his soul. And he had found this peace in a hut on the bank of the Ganges, at Rishi Kesh, where he had decided to settle some seven years before my arrival there. To say he settled is only a manner of speaking; for six months out of the year he was on the road, either climbing up towards the snow-covered peaks of Badrinath, or going down to Pondicherry or Rameshvaram.

One evening, when the two of us were taking a walk upstream along the river, among the rocks which tumble down from the mountains on the north to the very edge of Rishi Kesh, I took him into my confidence and told him about the occurrence in which I had been an involuntary participant. I had gone to visit him in his hut, as usual, right after supper, and then we had set out towards Lakshmanjula, slowly, keeping as close to the water's edge as we could. After hearing my tale, he turned towards me with a smile and asked, "And have you found some explanation for this unusual happening?"

I replied that I had tried quite a number of explanations, but

53

that none of them satisfied me completely. Of one thing I was sure: that everything that had happened to us was, of course, due to the fact that we had without knowing it approached too close to the place where Suren Bose was performing a secret ritual that night.

"But I don't understand," I continued, "how we, who were, after all, at Budge's bungalow, could be close enough to him to interfere with the awful ritual which he had started. It may be that the sacred zone created for such a ritual—which, I have no doubt, makes use of exceptional magical powers, and which probably requires a setting at once terrifying and obscene—it may be that this zone covers a very large area. In any case, whether we really did leave in the car, and *crossed through* the ritual zone, or else came too close to it; or whether we never left at all, as the chauffeur and all the other servants at the bungalow maintain, the fact is that in one way or another we interrupted Bose in the midst of his meditation. And then, in order not to be disturbed, Bose cast us, by means of his occult powers, into another *space* and another *time;* in other words, he projected us into an episode which had taken place some hundred and fifty years ago in the vicinity of Serampore, and we became witnesses, you might say, to the murder of Dāsa's young wife . . ."

I looked at Swami Shivananda, and I thought I detected a very discreet smile on his lips.

"I believe such a thing to be possible," I went on. "I believe that someone who is endowed with great occult powers can remove you from the *present,* can annul your present condition, and can project you anywhere in the universe. But what baffles me is another detail . . ."

Swami Shivananda turned towards me with a laugh and took my hand.

"Is it really only this 'other detail' that baffles you in the whole occurrence you have related to me?"

"To be quite frank," I admitted, "there are a number of minor details that I don't understand. For instance, I don't really know whether we actually left in the car, or whether we were subject to an illusion from the very beginning, even before we left the bungalow. If we really left, then I don't understand when the spell first came over us; probably it was a few minutes after our departure, as soon as we came close, shall we say, to the sacred zone of Bose's ritual and meditation. But then, what happened to the chauffeur? Was he too under the spell, for a time, and did he then recover, see that we were no longer in the car, and return to the bungalow, where he got ready to put on an act and persuaded the other servants to say that he had never even stirred from in front of the veranda? Or, was he under the spell and did he come back without being aware of it, resuming his former position in front of the veranda, and did he then wake up from the spell without remembering anything of what he had done? Such would be the possibilities on the first hypothesis—that we really did leave Budge's bungalow. But I have also considered a second hypothesis: that we never left at all, that we only had the illusion of starting off in the car, and that in actual fact the spell overcame us without our ever leaving the bungalow. I reasoned like this: whether Suren Bose *felt* our presence, and then, in order to keep us at a distance from the scene of his awful ceremony, cast a spell over us—or whether simply carrying out this secret ritual unleashed forces which, without any express intention on his part, projected us into another space and time, it remains a distinct possibility that all of us could have been 'enchanted' even before getting in the car. But then, how can I explain the fact that the rest of them—the servants—were not affected by the spell? How can I explain the fact that I got the feeling of something strange going on only some time after lighting the cigarette, in the car, and then only after I became convinced that I didn't recognize the countryside? And then, how *did* we leave the bungalow? For there can be no slightest doubt that we *did leave,* that we wandered through the jungle, and came back along a dusty road, with our clothing dirty and torn. The best proof of this was the tracks which Budge's chauffeur discovered the next day. But these tracks too puzzle me greatly; they didn't fade away in the woods, as you might have expected, but vanished in the middle of a field—and we can't remember crossing any other field but the one in front of Nīlāmvara Dāsa's house . . ."

Swami Shivananda was listening to me attentively, but his face was lit up with the same kind and understanding smile.

"I must say you reason like a regular detective," he said, with another laugh.

"And I reason that way because I have a special theory about miracles," I answered, "but what happened at Serampore was *not* a miracle, but only the play of certain magical forces of a lower, demonic nature."

"Tantra does not admit of any moral distinctions among the magical forces you are speaking of," he interrupted me. "In this respect it resembles your physics, with its European concepts of the objective nature of force."

But I was eager to hear from his lips the explanation of these events, and wasn't in the least disposed to listen to a discourse on the similarities or differences between Tantra and European science. So I interrupted him.

"Whatever may be the truth about our *leaving* the bungalow, that is not what puzzles me the most. What really baffles me is another circumstance, to which I referred just a moment ago, and which I shall now tell you about. I can accept the fact that we were projected out of the real time and space, and that we became witnesses to a crime committed a hundred and fifty years ago in the very same place. The forest which we saw from a certain moment on was the forest *of those days*—vast, with ancient tall trees, which were no doubt cut down in the course of the last century. Similarly, Nīlāmvara's house was an eighteenth-century house, one of the villas which we later learned he possessed in the vicinity of Serampore, and which subsequently was razed to the ground. The men we saw there, carrying the body of young Lila on a bier made of branches, were likewise dressed in eighteenth-century fashion, with turbans and shalwars, such as are now no longer worn in Bengal. All of this I understand very well. And I wouldn't be so puzzled if the three of us had merely found ourselves *present* at the murder of Lila and at the grief in Dāsa's house. But all we did was *hear* the young woman's screams, and although we went running all around, we didn't *see* anyone at all, neither her nor those who had abducted her. And then, I can't make any sense at all out of everything that happened after we entered Dāsa's house. I could understand it if, as I said, we had witnessed his grief of a hundred and fifty years ago—just that and nothing more. But that's not what happened: this was not a simple repetition of the events which occurred a hundred and fifty years ago; quite the contrary—new elements were interjected, created by *our* presence in that house. We talked with Dāsa, and he answered us. He even told Bogdanof that he didn't understand English. None of these things happened a hundred and fifty years ago. Thus we were not purely and simply *present* at a scene which occurred long ago; we ourselves actually *took part* in this scene, modifying it by our presence, of which the participants took note, and by our questions, which they answered. To be sure, we were struck by the fact that those two individuals, the old servant and Nīlāmvara, seemed unnaturally stiff. Now if Chatterji had told us that they both died that same night when Lila was murdered, then I might think that what we saw was their spectral forms, as they appeared at the moment of death. But Dāsa continued to live after the death of his wife, and it is to be supposed that the servant lived for some time longer too. Thus the way they looked as we saw them that night was not the way they looked at the time of their deaths, many years later. So then what is the explanation for their preternatural stiffness? It can't have been rigor mortis, for *they* were not affected by that as a result of the episode which we witnessed —the killing of Lila. We didn't, then, have a direct experience of an incident *just as it happened* a hundred and fifty years ago; rather, we were projected as witnesses to an event of that time, but an event which *we modified*. This is truly beyond the limits of all human understanding; for while my mind can accept the hypothesis that, thanks to certain unknown forces, I am able to abolish time and be present at a past event—the same mind refuses to accept the possibility that I could modify the structure and appearance of that event. I accept the hypothesis that I could be present at the Battle of Waterloo, but I cannot believe that I could be present at the Battle of Waterloo and see Napoleon emerge from it victorious . . ."

Swami Shivananda began to laugh, and took me by the arm.

"Your reasoning is all very fine, and yet it's completely wrong just the same," he said to me. "But come, why don't we walk a little farther on?" he suddenly asked me, pulling me along with him.

I followed him, and leaving the bank of the Ganges, we slowly began to climb the path towards the woods.

"And it's wrong," he continued, "because it attributes a certain *reality* to events, whether these events are past, present, or future.

But no event in our world is *real*, my friend. Everything that occurs in this universe is *illusory*. Not only the death of Lila and her husband's grief, but also the encounter between you, living men, and their shades—all these things are illusory. And in a world of appearances, in which no thing and no event has any permanence, any reality of its own—whoever is master of certain forces can do anything he wishes. Obviously he doesn't create anything real either, but only a play of appearances."

"I don't understand," I admitted in confusion. "Everything in the world is illusory, granted, but even these illusions have certain laws of their own which give them an appearance of consistency."

"Illusions and appearances obey the laws you speak of only for the one who *believes* in those laws," Swami Shivananda continued. "But it would seem that Suren Bose, and perhaps not he alone, didn't believe in the 'laws' which govern the universe of illusions and appearances . . ."

Seeing that I continued to stand there with my eyes cast down, still unconvinced by his arguments, he squeezed my arm harder and pulled me along.

"Come, I'll show you . . ."

At that moment, I suddenly felt my cheeks burn, and my breath almost stopped in my breast. I staggered, and certainly would have fallen down if I had not been held up by the strong arm of Swami Shivananda. I seemed to be in another world. The coolness of the Himalayan night had disappeared as if by magic, giving place to the warm, humid night of the southern regions. I couldn't understand what was happening to me, and fearfully I raised my eyes from the ground.

I paled when I saw an immense forest all around me. Swami Shivananda made me walk rapidly, without saying a word to me. But all at once I recognized where we were; I caught sight of the glowing embers in the abandoned charcoal-kilns, and not far ahead of us I saw the house of Nīlāmvara. The blood drained from my cheeks, and although my companion tried to hold on to me, I wrenched my arm from his grasp and fell at his feet.

"I can't stand this any longer, Swami!" I cried. "Wake me up! I can't stand going through the whole business a second time . . ."

I don't remember what happened then. When I woke up, the next day, in my *kutiar*, the sun was high in the sky, and the green waters of the Ganges seemed to me gentle beyond words, incomparably clear and soothing.

The Secret of Dr. Honigberger

1.

ONE morning in the autumn of 1934 a messenger brought me a very strange letter, and said that he was to wait for an immediate reply. A lady named Zerlendi, whom I had never heard of, was writing to invite me to visit her that very afternoon. The letter was very proper and couched in extremely polite terms, as was customary in our parents' day when a lady was writing to a stranger. "I understand that you have recently returned from the Orient," she wrote among other things, "and I thought you might be interested in taking a look at the collections made by my husband."

I must confess that at that time I was not in the least interested in the many acquaintances I was invited to make just because I had spent several years in the Orient. More than once I felt obliged to renounce a friendship which in other respects promised to be a very pleasant one, simply because I would not consent to utter platitudes about the "mysteries of Asia," about fakirs, wonders, or adventures in the jungle, about which I would be expected to supply all sorts of sensational details. Mrs. Zerlendi's letter, however, had mentioned certain oriental collections, but without saying anything about their nature or origin, and that was enough to arouse my curiosity.

I did take a real interest in the life of those Rumanians who had succumbed to a passion for the Orient. In this connection I might mention that, many years before this incident, at one of the booksellers on the Dâmbovitza Quai, I had come across a whole chest of books on China; they had all been carefully studied, for their former owner had annotated them and sometimes even corrected them in pencil; most of them bore his signature on the flyleaf: Radu C. And this Radu C. was no dilettante: his books, which are now in my possession, were proof that he had undertaken a serious and disciplined study of the Chinese language. Thus, he had annotated the six volumes of the *Mémoires historiques de Se-Ma-Ts'ien* in the translation of Edouard Chavannes, and had corrected all the typographical errors in the Chinese text; he knew the Chinese classics in Couvreur's editions, he subscribed to the review *T'oung Pao,* and he had bought all the volumes of the *Variétés sinologiques* which had appeared in Shanghai up to the beginning of the war. This man interested me from the time I acquired part of his library, although it was a long time before I learned his full name. The bookseller had bought several hundred of his books around 1920, and except for a few illustrated volumes which he had sold again immediately, he had never been able to interest anyone in this collection of sinological texts and studies.

I wondered at the time who this Rumanian could have been, who had been so devoted to the study of Chinese, and who had left behind him not a single trace, not even his full name. What dark passion had borne him to that distant shore, a shore he desired to approach not as a mere dilettante, but whose language he wanted to learn, and whose history he was striving to master? And did he ever succeed in reaching China, or had he perished before his time during the war, in some miserable hole at the front?

Much later I was to get an answer to some of the questions I asked myself as I stood there, intrigued and pensive, leafing through his books at the shop on the quai. An answer, incidentally, which was itself wrapped in unexpected mysteries. But that is another story entirely, and has no connection with the events I am about to describe. But recalling this Radu C., and a few other orientalists and oriental enthusiasts who had lived here in Rumania, unknown to anyone, I decided to accept the lady's invitation.

That same afternoon I set out for the house, which was on S. Street. Stopping at No. 17, I saw before me one of those houses that I never can pass by without pausing for a closer look, trying to divine what is going on behind those ancient walls, wondering who lives there and what destiny he is working out. S. Street is right in the heart of Bucharest, not far from Calea Victoriei. By what miracle had the boyar's house at No. 17 been preserved—with its ironwork fence and its gravel-strewn yard, with its façade partly overshadowed by acacias and chestnuts grown wild? The gate opened with difficulty, and between beds gay with autumn flowers I saw a pool in which the water had long since dried up, and two garden dwarfs with the coloring faded from their heads. The very air seemed to be different here. A world which was slowly disappearing from the other proud quarters of the capital was here preserved with decency, without having to undergo the agony of degeneration and impoverishment. It was an old-time boyar's house, but well preserved, except that moisture from the trees had caused the façade to fade prematurely. The main entrance was protected by a sunroof of frosted glass, such as was common forty years ago. A few stone steps, green with moss, with great vases of flowers at the sides, led up to a porch with upper windowpanes of colored glass. There was no nameplate on the bell.

I was expected. An old housemaid with a limp let me in at once and showed me into a huge parlor. I had scarcely time to cast a quick glance at the furniture and the pictures around me when Mrs. Zerlendi entered through an oaken door. She was a woman of over fifty, but one whom you could hardly have forgotten even after meeting her only once. She did not age like everyone else, this lady. Or, perhaps, she aged in the same way as women of former centuries, who understood in some mysterious way that through death you will approach the grand revelation of all meaning, rather than just the end of an earthly life, the gradual drying up of the flesh and its final absorption into the earth. I have always divided people into two categories: those who understand death as an *end* to life and the body, and those who conceive it as the *beginning* of a new, spiritual existence. And I never form an opinion of any man I meet until I have learned his honest belief about death. Otherwise I might be deceived by high intelligence and dazzling charm.

Mrs. Zerlendi sat down in an armchair, and, with a gesture that was free of the familiarity common to women of a certain age, motioned me to a wooden chair with a high back.

"I thank you for coming," she said. "My husband would have been delighted to meet you. He too loved India, perhaps more than befitted his profession as a doctor . . ."

I was prepared to hear a long story, and I was glad that meanwhile I would be able to study attentively the strange face of Mrs. Zerlendi without appearing to be impertinent. But my hostess was silent for a few moments, and then asked me, with her head slightly inclined towards me, "Are you familiar with the life and writings of Dr. Johann Honigberger?

"My husband became enamored of India through the books of

this Transylvanian German doctor from Brashov. He no doubt inherited an interest in history, for history was the passion of his whole family; but he only began to study India after discovering the works of Dr. Honigberger. Indeed, for some years he did nothing but collect materials on him, and he even began a monograph on this Transylvanian German doctor. He was a physician himself, and so he felt qualified to write such a work."

I must admit that at that time I knew very little about Dr. Johann Honigberger. I recalled reading, many years before, his principal work, *Thirty-five Years in the East,* in an English translation, the only one which had been available to me in Calcutta. At that time I was studying yoga philosophy and techniques, and I consulted Honigberger's book especially for the details it gave on these occult practices, with which, it appears, the doctor had a firsthand acquaintance. Since the book had appeared, however, around the middle of the last century, I suspected the author of a certain lack of critical spirit. I did not know then, though, that this doctor, who enjoyed such a great reputation in oriental studies, came from an old Brashov family. But now it was precisely this detail that interested me.

". . . My husband carried on an extensive correspondence with a number of doctors and scholars who had known Honigberger, for although the latter died in 1869 in Brashov, soon after returning from his last trip to India, there were still quite a few people alive who had known him. One of his sons had attained the position of magistrate in Iassy—he was a child of the doctor's first marriage; but my husband never managed to meet him, although he made a number of trips to Iassy in search of certain papers . . ."

Involuntarily I began to smile. I was surprised that Mrs. Zerlendi knew such precise details of Honigberger's biography. She must have guessed my thoughts, for she added, "These things interested *him* so much that they have been forever impressed on my mind. These things, and many others . . ."

She suddenly fell silent, lost in thought. I later had opportunity to learn how many and how precise were the facts Mrs. Zerlendi knew about Dr. Honigberger. She spent one entire evening telling me about his first stay in India, after he had spent some four years in Asia Minor, a year in Egypt, and seven years in Syria. Mrs. Zerlendi's knowledge was easily explained, however, for she had gone through her husband's books and manuscripts several times, as though she had at some time nourished the wish to bring to a successful conclusion the work in which he had been interrupted.

The fact is that it is difficult to escape the mysterious fascination of this Transylvanian doctor (who was a doctor only by his own authority, for officially all he held was a pharmacist's diploma). Honigberger had spent more than half of his long life in the Orient. At one time he served as court physician, pharmacist, director of the arsenal, and admiral to Maharaja Ranjit Singh in Lahore. Several times he amassed considerable fortunes, and then lost them again. He was an adventurer in the grand manner, but he was never a charlatan. He was acquainted with a great many branches of knowledge, both profane and occult, and his ethnographical, botanical, numismatic, and artistic collections have enriched many famous museums. It is easy to understand why Dr. Zerlendi, with his passionate interest in our people's past and in the history of medicine, should have devoted so many years of his life to digging out and trying to make sense of the *true* facts of Honigberger's biography.

"For he early became convinced," Mrs. Zerlendi once told me, "that Honigberger's life had a great many hidden mysteries, for all the books that have been written about him. For example, he couldn't account for his last trip to India, in 1858, when he was in a very precarious state of health, after returning gravely ill from an expedition to tropical Africa. Why did Honigberger return to India again, exhausted as he was, and why did he die as soon as he set foot in Brashov again, my husband kept asking himself. Furthermore, the doctor's so-called botanical explorations in Kashmir, carried out long before, looked suspicious to him. He had reason to think that in reality Honigberger had not only been in Kashmir but had also entered Tibet, or, in any case, had studied the science of occult pharmacology in one of those monasteries in the Himalayas, and that the botanical investigations had been only a pretext. As to that, however, *you* are in a better position to judge," Mrs. Zerlendi had added.

I must admit that I too became convinced that the life of the Transylvanian doctor was wrapped in mystery, after I had gone through the books and documents concerning Honigberger which Mrs. Zerlendi's husband had collected with such great care. But everything which followed my first visit to the house on S. Street far surpassed the mystery of Honigberger.

"I thought at the time," Mrs. Zerlendi recommenced after a long pause, "that it would be a pity for all this work to be wasted. I heard someone speak of you, and I have read some of your works, especially those concerned with India and Indian philosophy. I can't say that I entirely understood them, but there was one thing I did understand: that I can turn to you with confidence . . ."

I tried to say that I was flattered, and so on, but Mrs. Zerlendi went right on in the same tone.

"For a good many years now hardly anyone has entered this house. No one but a few friends, who lack my husband's special training. So his desk and his library have remained unchanged since 1910. I myself was abroad for a long time, and after my return I was careful not to mention my husband's name too often. His medical colleagues considered him quite mad at that time. The library that I'm now going to show you has been seen by only one other person really able to appreciate it, and that was Bucura Dumbrava.[1] I wrote to her just as I did to you, saying that I had a valuable oriental collection, and she came, though only after a long delay. I think she was quite interested in it. She told me that she had found here books which she had once looked for in vain in the British Museum. But she didn't have time to examine the library at her leisure. She took a few notes, and she promised to come back again after her return from India. As you may perhaps know, she was going to India for a Theosophical Congress. But she never again set foot on Rumanian soil. She died at Port Said."

I don't know whether Mrs. Zerlendi attached any secret significance to her dying on the eve of returning home. She fell silent again and seemed to be looking at me with eager expectation. I felt that I had to say something too, so I said that mystery is so active in our existence that it's not at all necessary to go looking for it far away, say in Adyar or Port Said. Mrs. Zerlendi made no reply. She got up from her chair and invited me to follow her into the library. As we were crossing the parlor I asked her whether her husband had ever been in India.

"That's hard to say," she whispered hesitantly, but with an attempt at a smile.

1. Bucura Dumbrava, d. 1926, was a writer and the founder of the Theosophical Society in Rumania (translator's note).

2.

I HAVE seen many libraries belonging to men of wealth and learning, but not one of them ever held such an allure for me as the
one on S. Street. When the massive oak door opened, I remained
transfixed on the threshold. It was one of those immense rooms
such as you rarely find even in the most sumptuous houses of
the last century. Large windows looked out on the garden in
back of the house. The curtains had been drawn back before we
came in, and the clear light of the autumn twilight made the
atmosphere of this room, with its high ceiling and its walls lined
with books, even more solemn. A wooden gallery ran around
the greater part of the library. There were perhaps thirty thousand volumes, most of them bound in leather, from the most
diverse branches of culture: medicine, history, religion, travel,
occultism, Indology. Mrs. Zerlendi led me straight to the shelves
which were entirely devoted to the books dealing with India.
Seldom have I found in a private collection such valuable books
in such great numbers. Only later, after I had spent an entire
afternoon before those bookshelves, was I able to get any adequate idea of what treasures were stored there. There were
hundreds of volumes of travels in India, from Marco Polo and

Tavernier down to Pierre Loti and Jaccolliot. It was obvious that Dr. Zerlendi had collected every sort of book published on India, for that is the only way I can account for the presence of certain impostors, for example, Louis Jaccolliot. Then there were complete sets of the *Journal Asiatique* and the *Journal of the Royal Asiatic Society* of London, not to mention the transactions of a great many academies, and hundreds of learned memoirs on the languages, literatures, and religions of India. All the outstanding publications of the last century in the realm of Indology were there, from the great St. Petersburg dictionary to the editions of Sanskrit texts published in Calcutta or Benares. What surprised me most was to see those volumes of Sanskrit texts.

"He began the study of Sanskrit in 1901," Mrs. Zerlendi explained, seeing my amazement, "and he acquired a thorough knowledge of it, as much as it is possible to learn far from the living centers of the language . . ."

And in fact, there were not only elementary books and even texts which a novice might buy, but also books which would be ordered only by someone who has penetrated deep into the secrets of the Sanskrit language. I found, for example, difficult commentaries such as the *Siddānta Kaumudī,* which indicated an interest in the nuances of Sanskrit grammar, the voluminous treatise of Medhaditi on the Laws of Manu, those thorny sub-commentaries to the Vedic texts which are published by the presses in Allahabad and Benares, and numerous books on Indian rituals. I was struck in particular by the presence of volumes on Indian medicine and of treatises on mysticism and asceticism. I knew from my own limited experience how unfathomable and difficult such texts are—they cannot be understood at all without a detailed commentary, and more often than not they are only half intelligible until they have been explained orally by a teacher.

I looked at Mrs. Zerlendi in amazement. I had entered the library with eager anticipation, expecting to find an extensive collection of materials on the life and works of Dr. Honigberger, and now I discovered the library of a learned Indologist, which in its immensity and variety would have made a Roth, a Jacobi, or a Sylvain Lévi jealous.

"It was his work on Honigberger that first aroused his interest in all this," explained Mrs. Zerlendi, guessing my thoughts, and she indicated another corner of the library, where I was shortly to see the books and documents concerning the Transylvanian doctor.

"But when did he have time to collect so many books, and how could he ever read them all?" I exclaimed in amazement.

"A good part of them he inherited from the family, particularly the history books," she said. "The rest he bought himself, especially during his last eight years. He sold some of our land . . ."

She uttered the last words with a smile and without the slightest trace of regret.

"All the bookdealers of Leipzig, Paris, and London knew him," she continued. "And he for his part knew something about buying books. Sometimes he bought whole libraries from the estates of deceased orientalists. But of course he didn't have time to read them all, although in his last years he used to stay up most of the night—he used to sleep only two or three hours."

"That must have ruined his health," I said.

"No, on the contrary," replied Mrs. Zerlendi. "He had an enormous capacity for work. And he followed a special regimen: he ate no meat at all, didn't smoke, drank no alcohol, tea, or coffee . . ."

I thought she was going to say something further, but she broke off suddenly and led me to the other end of the library, where the "Honigberger corner" was. Here were all the books of the Transylvanian doctor, and a good many of the works which had been published about his amazing life. In one corner there was a copy of Mahlknecht's engraving, the famous engraving which shows Honigberger in his costume as a councilor of Ranjit Singh. There were boxes in which Dr. Zerlendi had collected countless letters from Honigberger to the scholars of his day, copies of portraits and engravings of his family and friends, and maps on which he had traced all of Honigberger's travels in Asia and Africa. Pensively I leafed through all these documents, whose true value I was only later to appreciate; I was amazed that such a man could have lived in our city only a quarter of a century earlier, without anyone suspecting the existence of the treasure he had collected.

"And why didn't he write the book about Honigberger?" I asked.

"He had started to write it," Mrs. Zerlendi said after a long pause, "but then he suddenly stopped, without ever telling me the real reason. As I told you, he carried on an extensive correspondence in his quest for information and unpublished documents. In 1906, on the occasion of the World's Fair, he met a friend of Constantin Honigberger's, the doctor's son by his first marriage, who had in his possession some letters and other papers, which by some chance had come into his custody. That same autumn my husband took a trip to Iassy, and he came back quite agitated. I don't think he had actually obtained the originals, but he had made copies of all those documents. In any case, from then on he gave up working on the book, and he applied himself more and more ardently to the study of Indian philosophy. In time Honigberger was quite forgotten, and in the years that followed my husband devoted himself exclusively to the study of Sanskrit."

With a smile she motioned to the walls of the library, the sight of which had at first so amazed me.

"And he never told you what led him to abandon the fruits of the work which had engrossed him for so many years?" I asked.

"He only hinted at it," began Mrs. Zerlendi, "for after his return from Iassy he became more taciturn. He told me once that it was essential for him to become thoroughly familiar with Indian philosophy and occultism in order to understand a certain phase of Honigberger's life, which up to that time had remained obscure and wrapped in legends. At the time when he started studying Sanskrit, he also became interested in occultism. But this is an episode which is very hazy to me, for my husband never spoke to me about this last passion of his. Instead, I could only guess how much these studies meant to him from the books he was constantly ordering. However, you can judge for yourself," Mrs. Zerlendi added, leading me to another part of the library.

I can't really say that at this point my surprise became any greater. Everything Mrs. Zerlendi had told me since we entered the library, everything I had so far seen, had held so many surprises and had increased my bewilderment to such a point that I examined the new shelves dumbly, overcome with wonder and admiration. You could see at first glance that the doctor had made an auspicious beginning in his collection of occult books. Missing were all those works of popularization with which French publishers in particular had flooded the market at the end of the last century. Missing too were the greater part of the theosophical books, most of which are mediocre and unreliable. There were, however, some of the books of Leadbeater and Annie Besant, together with the complete works of Mme Blavatsky, which Dr. Zerlendi had read with special attention, as I was able to convince myself on another occasion. On the other hand, in addition to Fabre d'Olivet and Rudolf Steiner, Stanislas de Guaita and Hartmann, the library was extremely rich in the classics of occultism, hermeticism, and traditional theosophy. Old editions of Swedenborg, Paracelsus, Cornelius Agrippa, Böhme, Della Riviera, and Pernety stood next to the works ascribed to Pythagoras, the hermetic texts, and the collections of famous alchemists, both in the old printings of Salmon and Manget and in the modern edition of Berthelot. Not even the forgotten books on physiognomy, astrology, and chiromancy were missing.

Later, when I had the opportunity to examine these shelves at my leisure, I discovered a number of extremely rare works, for instance the *De Aqua Vitae Simplici et Composita* of Arnauld de Villeneuve, or Christian apocrypha such as that *Adam and Eve* for which Strindberg searched for so long. It became clear that Dr. Zerlendi had been guided by a fixed idea and a precise goal in assembling this fine occult library. As I discovered little by little, not a single important author, not a single noteworthy book was missing. It was clear that the doctor was seeking more than merely superficial information, that he wanted to assimilate the essential points of occult doctrines and terminology, so that he could speak of them with some authority in the biography of Honigberger on which he was working. His books showed me that he wanted to satisfy himself as to the truth which is preserved, well-hidden though it be, in the hermetic tradition. Otherwise, there would have been no point in his reading Agrippa von Nettesheim and the *Bibliotheca Chemica Curiosa*.

And it was precisely this lively interest of the doctor's in occultism, together with his passion for Indian philosophy, and in particular for the secret sects in India, that made me extremely curious, the more so as Mrs. Zerlendi had given me to understand that this new and final passion of her husband's had taken possession of him as a result of his trip to Iassy.

"I don't suppose he was content merely to read occult works," I said. "No doubt the doctor must have tried some of the exercises for himself."

"I assume as much," said Mrs. Zerlendi after a few moments of hesitation. "Though he never told me anything about it. But in his last years he spent almost all his time in this study or alone on one of our estates in Oltenia. As I told you, he never showed any sign of weariness, despite his almost ascetic life. On the contrary, I might even say he felt better than ever before."

And yet he died just the same, I said to myself, as I listened to Mrs. Zerlendi's timid explanations. It had become almost dark in the room, and my hostess went with soft steps to turn on the lights. Two immense chandeliers, from which hung innumerable crystal arrowheads, flooded the library with an artificial light which seemed too bright. I couldn't bring myself to leave, and stood irresolute before the shelves with the books on occultism. Mrs. Zerlendi came back to where I was standing, after closing one of the windows—the one that opened onto a stone balcony —and drawing a curtain of green and gold velvet.

"Now that you have seen just what sort of collection this is," she began, "I can tell you what I have in mind. For many years now I have been asking myself whether I too don't have a certain responsibility towards the fruit of all my husband's work, these drawers full of papers and letters which he collected at the time when he was occupied with Honigberger's biography. I don't know exactly what he had decided to devote himself to in his last years, but the studies that he was then engaged in were begun in the first instance in order to understand Honigberger better. When I heard about you and learned that you had spent so many years in India studying Indian philosophy and religion, I thought that perhaps you already *knew* whatever it was that my husband wanted to learn, and that for you Honigberger's life might hold no secrets. Then all this work won't have been in vain," added Mrs. Zerlendi, waving her slender hand towards the "Honigberger corner." "Perhaps you might be interested in writing the life of the Transylvanian doctor, which my husband was unable to finish. I would die happy," she continued, "in the knowledge that my husband's materials were of some use to someone, and that the biography of which he dreamed would someday see the light of day."

I didn't know what to say. Never before had I undertaken a commissioned work, and in a field with which I was not familiar. Nearly all the books I have written I turned out in haste, impelled by the demands of life—but always I have written what I chose to, whether I was commencing work on a novel or a philosophical treatise. I felt, though, that I shouldn't hesitate too long.

"My dear lady," I began, "I am flattered at the confidence you place in me, and I must admit that I am happy at the very thought that I shall be able to return to this library without inconveniencing you. I don't know, however, whether I shall ever be able to bring to a satisfactory conclusion the work your husband had started. In the first place, I'm not a doctor, and I know nothing about the history of medicine in the nineteenth century. And then, your husband had a good knowledge of a great many things which are completely foreign to me. But I can promise you one thing: that Honigberger's biography will be written and published. I might enlist the aid of someone who is well informed about everything concerning nineteenth-century medicine and history."

"The same idea has occurred to me," said Mrs. Zerlendi. "But the most important thing is not the medical part—for that I can always find qualified collaborators—but rather the orientalistic part of the biography. If I didn't know how much my husband wanted to have a critical biography of Honigberger written by a Rumanian—for there is no lack of biographies from the pens of foreigners—I would have turned to a specialist in England or Germany, where Honigberger is particularly well known."

She stopped suddenly, and after a few moments of silence she lifted her head and looked me in the eye.

"And then, I must admit there's one other thing, which may perhaps strike you as too personal: I have a great wish to be near at hand while this biography is being written. There are certain episodes in the life of this man which are quite mysterious, as you will see, and I keep hoping that someday someone will explain them to me."

3.

How right Mrs. Zerlendi was when she spoke of those mysterious episodes in the life of Johann Honigberger I found out later, when I read with close attention the manuscripts and documents which the doctor had collected, sorted out, and annotated. I returned to the house on S. Street a few days later, and from then on I spent at least three afternoons a week in the library. The autumn continued exceptionally beautiful and warm. I used to come around four o'clock and stay until late in the evening. Sometimes Mrs. Zerlendi would meet me in the parlor when I first came in. Usually, however, we met in the library, which she would enter a considerable time after I had settled down to work, approaching my desk with the same discreet grace and extending to me the same unusually pale hand from a black silk sleeve. Right behind her would come the aged housemaid with the tray with preserves and coffee. Mrs. Zerlendi never failed to be there when my coffee was served. No doubt she told herself that her presence wouldn't disturb me during that pause when I interrupted my work for a while, leaving the folder with manuscripts lying open before me.

"How is it going?" she would ask me every time. "Do you

think you'll be able to do something with my husband's papers?"

The work progressed very slowly, however. Perhaps this was my own fault, for I was not content to examine only the Honigberger materials; instead, at the same time that I was inventorying them, I was also going through the numberless shelves of Indological and occult books, and this was an occupation for which I developed a real passion, and one which took considerable time. After my fourth visit to the house on S. Street I finally found out how far the doctor had got with Honigberger's biography. The final draft broke off with Honigberger's return to Aleppo in 1822, where the Transylvanian doctor introduced the new methods of vaccination; there were several chapters more in rough draft covering the seven years he spent in Syria. But all this accounted for scarcely a quarter of the biography properly speaking, for Honigberger really became interesting only after his arrival at the court of Ranjit Singh. For the other periods in the life of the doctor-adventurer I found only documentary materials, filed away with care in boxes which were arranged in chronological order. The dates, places, and number of documents were marked on each filing-box. Sometimes there was a question mark beside the year, or a reference to a separate file of apocryphal documents. For Dr. Zerlendi had become convinced —as he pointed out in a footnote to the first chapter of the biography—that many of Honigberger's statements, which had been accepted without question by his contemporary biographers, were based on false data or on documents which were purposely falsified later on. What possible interest Honigberger could have had in misrepresenting a life which was quite fabulous enough as it was, and stamped from first to last with the sign of mystery and adventure, I never quite understood.

"Haven't you yet come to the mysteries my husband told me about?" Mrs. Zerlendi asked me one day.

81

I found it difficult to answer. I could guess what sort of revelations the old lady expected me to make, and I didn't know whether I would ever be able to make them. The cases of suspended animation, of yogic trance, of levitation, imperviousness to fire, and invisibility to which Honigberger referred, and which Dr. Zerlendi had studied with special attention, were very difficult to explain to anyone who did not understand *theoretically* that such things can actually occur. And when it came to Honigberger's mysterious journeys to Kashmir and Tibet, his researches on magical pharmacology, and the possibility that he had taken part in certain initiation ceremonies of the Vallabhacharya sect—I myself was still in the dark. If Dr. Zerlendi ever learned anything definite about these mysterious episodes, he left no record of it in the biographical files.

"I encounter mysteries at every step," I answered evasively. "But I haven't yet been able to find any way to explain them . . ."

Mrs. Zerlendi continued to stand there beside me for a few moments with a faraway look in her eyes; then she gradually collected her thoughts and left the library with her melancholy step. Whenever she lingered a bit longer to talk, she would ask me about my travels in India; she was particularly eager to hear all about the monasteries I had visited in the Himalayas—something I am always reluctant to speak of. She never told me anything about her life or her family. I never even heard the names of the friends of whom she sometimes spoke.

Everything I found out later I stumbled on by accident. Once, three weeks after my first visit, I arrived a little earlier than usual. It was raining that day, a mournful autumn rain, and it was some time before the aged housemaid came to let me in. Mrs. Zerlendi was ill, she said. But I was to come in just the same; she had even made a fire in the fireplace. I entered with a feeling of diffidence. The library seemed changed in the murky light of the autumn rain. The fireplace couldn't warm all of this immense room. Nevertheless I set to work with a will. I had a feeling that Mrs. Zerlendi might bear her suffering more easily in the knowledge that I was there at work in a nearby room, and that perhaps someday quite soon I would be able to explain to her some of the "mysteries" which her husband had uncovered.

Half an hour after my arrival the door of the library opened and a young lady with a cigarette in her hand entered. She didn't seem in the least surprised to find me there at the desk with the file folders open before me.

"Oh, so it's you!" she exclaimed, coming over to the desk.

I got up and introduced myself.

"I know—Mother has told me about you," she replied. Then she added, "Let's hope that you have more luck."

I smiled in confusion, not knowing just what I should say. Then I began to talk about everything I had discovered regarding Honigberger. The young lady looked at me ironically.

"I've heard all that long ago," she interrupted me. "The *others* too got that far. Poor Hans got even further, they say . . ."

My astonishment must have showed in my face, for the young lady began to laugh. She put out her cigarette in a copper ashtray and came closer.

"Or did you perhaps imagine that these 'mysteries' had been waiting a quarter of a century for *you* to solve them? A mistaken idea, my dear sir! Others have tried it before you. Father was, after all, a man of some prominence, and his 'case' was not soon forgotten among a fairly large group of people in the prewar years."

"If you have caught me in error, it's not my fault," I answered, striving to appear as little agitated as possible. "Mrs. Zerlendi thought best to disclose to me certain things only, and to keep silent about others. In any case, my task is quite limited in scope,"

83

I added with a smile. "I am here to look over the documentary materials relating to the biography of Dr. Honigberger."

The young lady looked me straight in the eye, as if she found it difficult to believe me. I was now able to take a better look at her. Tall, slender—almost thin, indeed—she had eyes which burned with a smoldering glow, and a nervous mouth. She wore no makeup at all, and this added a few years to the thirty or more she actually counted.

"I suspected that Mother was concealing certain things from you," she began in a voice less tense than before. "But perhaps otherwise you would have been disillusioned from the very beginning, if she had told you that your present work had already been performed by three other people. The last one was a German officer who remained in Bucharest after the occupation. 'Poor Hans,' we called him, for his fate was truly tragic. He died from a hunting accident on one of our estates. He claimed that he was beginning to understand the Honigberger 'mysteries' to which Father referred, but he said he knew too little Rumanian, and that he had to learn more. I don't quite understand what improving his Rumanian had to do with the Honigberger 'mysteries.' In my opinion he didn't find out much either."

"Nothing that you have told me," I began, "discourages me in the least. On the contrary, it only makes me feel even closer to this Honigberger, though until a few weeks ago his name meant no more to me than that of some globe-trotting adventurer."

The young lady smiled again and sat down in the armchair beside the desk, continuing to look at me searchingly.

"Mother is less interested in Honigberger than you suppose," she said. "What she is most of all interested in is finding out what happened to Father . . ."

"I have come to realize that," I interrupted her. "And since I never dared to ask *her* about it, I must ask *you* to enlighten me.

84

What did your father die of, and under what circumstances?"

The young lady sat hesitating for a few moments, with bowed head. She seemed to be considering whether she should tell me the truth, or whether it might not be better for me to learn it by myself, from some other source. At last she slowly got up from the chair and spoke.

"Father didn't die. At least, we don't know whether or when he died. On the 10th of September, 1910, he disappeared from home; since that time no one has ever seen him again, and we have never heard anything about him."

The two of us gazed at each other in silence. I didn't know what to say. I didn't even know whether she was telling me the whole truth or whether she was holding back certain painful details. She opened a small amber cigarette case and took out a cigarette.

"No doubt he set out for the Orient, for India," I said, in order to break the silence. "On Honigberger's trail . . ."

"That's what we thought too. That is, that's what our friends thought, for I was then in the second grade and didn't quite understand what had happened. I came home from school and found everybody upset and frightened. Father had disappeared that morning, or perhaps during the night."

"He probably wanted to leave without saying anything ahead of time," I said. "He foresaw the difficulties he would encounter if he told anyone what he planned to do."

"Of course. But it's very difficult to accept the idea that he could leave for the Orient without a passport, without money, without clothing . . ."

I didn't understand, and she continued.

"The fact is that Father *disappeared*, in the true sense of the word. And he disappeared without taking with him a single suit of clothes, without a hat, and leaving all his money behind in the

85

desk drawer. He took no papers with him, didn't get out his passport, and didn't even write a letter to Mother or any of his friends. You can't imagine how mysterious this disappearance seemed to those who knew the circumstances. Father had for some years been leading a very strange, almost ascetic life. He saw no one. His days and nights he spent in this library and in his bedroom, where he slept only two hours a night on a wooden pallet without a mattress and without a pillow. He dressed very simply in white trousers, sandals, and a linen shirt. That's all he wore around the house summer and winter. And in this costume, in which he wouldn't have gone out in the street, he *disappeared*. I have been unable to learn whether he disappeared during the night, leaving right from here, from the library, or after retiring to his room. Everyone in the house was usually asleep when he stopped working, at three in the morning. Two hours later, at five, he would wake up; he would take a shower, and then stay shut up in his room for a long time, meditating. That's what we thought, at least, for he never told Mother about it. He had cut himself off from the world and from his family. On the rare occasions when I saw him, I felt that his love for me was not dead, but it was a different kind of love . . ."

"And all inquiries came to nought?" I asked. "No trace of him has been found anywhere? It's incredible that a person can just disappear like that without leaving behind a trace of some sort."

"And yet that's just how it was. We never found the slightest indication that he had made any preparations for leaving. Everything was in order both here and in his bedroom; the books and notebooks were lying on this desk the same as every evening, and we found his watch, his keys, and his change purse on the night table in the bedroom. Just as if he had disappeared in the course of a few seconds, before he had time to get his things together or to write a word of explanation or apology . . ."

The young lady suddenly interrupted her confidences and extended her hand to me.

"Now that I've told you what you should have known from the beginning, I will leave you. I must only ask you not to mention our talk to Mother. She holds certain superstitious beliefs, and I don't want to provoke her by flouting them."

4.

She left before I could muster sufficient courage to stop her and ask the many questions her story had raised in my mind. For example, why there wasn't more talk at the time about this mysterious disappearance, or what had happened to the other people whom Mrs. Zerlendi had asked to examine the library, and who, as the young lady had remarked in passing, had had no luck? I sat down at the desk rather dazed from all I had heard. I couldn't collect my thoughts. I now looked at the folders in front of me and the books that surrounded me on all sides with new feelings. The admiration I had felt as a bibliophile and Indologist now gave place to a complex of feelings difficult to describe, but which included fear, disbelief, and fascination. I simply could not believe word for word all that my visitor had told me. Nevertheless, in the light of her revelations I now understood the old lady's reluctance to speak to me openly, the care she had taken never to mention her husband's death to me, and the curiosity which she could scarcely control.

I told myself that the reason Dr. Zerlendi's disappearance had seemed so incomprehensible was that the doctor must have been preparing for it well ahead of time, right down to the smallest detail, fired by the desire to get to India and make a complete break with his previous life. But it was just this carefully managed departure, the secrecy with which he had prepared for it, and his consuming passion for the mysteries of India that had fascinated me. I had never before heard of anyone who had planned such a sudden departure, without saying good-bye, without farewell letters, without leaving behind a trace of any sort. After all that I had heard, the Honigberger file still lying open on the desk no longer seemed very interesting to me. I went over to the shelves of books on Indology; I knew that was where the drawers were in which the doctor had kept his manuscripts and file cards, the evidence of so many years of study. I opened the first drawer and began listing its contents with great care, examining one notebook after another.

Here were the copybooks with his Sanskrit exercises, and old memories stirred in me as I gazed at the drills and declensions that I too had once grappled with: *nṛpaḥ, nṛpam, nṛjena, nṛpāya, nṛpāt, nṛpasya, nṛpe, nṛpa,* etc. You could see how awkwardly the doctor had written the Sanskrit letters. But he must have been a man of tremendous perseverance, for dozens of copybook pages were covered with the declension of one and the same word, repeated over and over again, like a school assignment. In another notebook he had progressed to whole sentences, most of them taken from the *Hitopadesha* and the *Panchatantra,* with the literal translation and a free translation alongside. I leafed through dozens of copybooks of this sort, filled to the last page with exercises, conjugations, declensions, or translations. In one thick notebook with alphabetical index-tabs the doctor had copied the new words he came across in his exercises. Some of the notebooks were dated on the flyleaf—probably an indication of when he had done the exercises they contained. I realized once again how much effort the doctor had devoted to the study of Sanskrit; one notebook of three hundred pages had been filled with exercises in less than two weeks.

On that rainy autumn afternoon I found nothing in the manuscript drawer to suggest anything more than a burning passion for the study of Sanskrit. There was just one simple note, on the first page of one of the exercise copybooks, that caught my attention for a moment. There were only a couple of words, but they filled me with excitement. *Shambala = Agarttha = the invisible realm.* All the rest of the pages were taken up with the usual schoolboy exercises.

I returned to the house the next day earlier than usual. Never before had I entered the library as excited and curious as I was now. I had spent almost the entire night mulling over the revelations Mrs. Zerlendi's daughter had made to me, asking myself what power from the beyond had impelled the doctor to commit so brutal a deed, to cut himself off so cruelly from his family, friends, and country. As soon as I entered the library I went straight to the drawers I had been going through the day before, took a whole armful of notebooks, folders, and copybooks, and sat down at the desk. This time I proceeded with the greatest of care. The notebooks were written in Sanskrit letters with an ever surer hand, which finally became cursive. Half an hour after my arrival Mrs. Zerlendi entered the library. She was pale and seemed feeble, although she had been ill only two days.

"I'm glad to see you working with such wholehearted interest," she began, glancing at the pile of notebooks. "These papers have never before been examined by anyone," she added, blushing slightly. "You mustn't pay any attention to what my daughter told you yesterday. Smaranda is an imaginative girl and fancies she sees connections between things which have nothing to do with each other. She was only a child at the time. And because Hans, her fiancé, died in a hunting accident after he too had begun looking through these notebooks, Smaranda has concocted a whole theory for herself. She believes there's a curse on everything connected with Honigberger, and that those who study the records on him, beginning with my husband, suffer all sorts of misfortunes—rather like the curse they say hangs over those who discovered Tutankhamun's tomb. But that's all just her imagination, and she only began to believe it after reading some books or other about Tutankhamun."

My bewilderment had increased still further as I listened to her. For now I didn't know what to believe, or on which side the truth lay. What Mrs. Zerlendi had told me about her daughter was all very confusing. And how did she know what the latter had told me? Surely she hadn't been listening at the door . . .

"Smaranda has never got over Hans' death, in 1921," Mrs. Zerlendi continued. "Perhaps it is because of this great sorrow that she sometimes seems to lack a sense of reality."

"But surely your daughter . . . ," I began, in an attempt to defend her.

"You needn't say anything more," Mrs. Zerlendi interrupted me. "I know what she thinks, and especially what she wants everyone she meets here in the library to think."

It seemed to me at the time that Mrs. Zerlendi's explanations were rather incoherent. However, she hadn't said anything about her husband. She hadn't asserted that he was dead, though she hadn't spoken of disappearance either. All she had tried to do was to defend herself against Smaranda's charge that she had invited others before me to try to explain the Honigberger "mysteries," which might also have been the mysteries of her husband.

"That's all I wanted to tell you," she whispered in a tired voice. "And now if you will excuse me, I must retire to my room. I'm still not entirely recovered."

91

Left to myself, I had to smile. I told myself that at any moment Smaranda was certain to enter the library and ask me not to believe what Mrs. Zerlendi had told me. But my curiosity was too strong, and after a while I resumed my perusal of the notebooks.

I continued looking through the notebooks until almost evening, but I didn't find anything else but translations, compositions, copies of texts, and textual and grammatical commentaries. One notebook, which contained notes on Vedanta philosophy and yoga, I thought might be more interesting, and I set it aside. Then I picked up a notebook with a black cardboard cover, which bore a notation and a serial number like all the others, and which in no way differed from them. The first page was taken up with a copy of some passages from the Upanishads. No doubt I would have assumed that the following pages contained more material of about the same kind, if my eye had not happened to fall on the first line of the second page: *ādau vāda āsīt, sa ca vāda īçvarābhimukha āsīt, sa ca vāda īçvara āsīt!* For an instant I didn't grasp the sense of the words, and I was about to turn the page when the translation of the sentence I had read suddenly burst on me. It was the prologue to the Gospel of John: "In the beginning was the Word, and the Word was with God, and the Word was God." I wondered why the doctor had copied this quotation in a Sanskrit translation, and I started to read further to try to discover the reason for it. But in the next instant excitement sent the blood rushing to my cheeks. The words which I was reading, in the strange dress of the Sanskrit letters, were Rumanian. "I begin this notebook on the 10th of January, 1908. The precaution I am taking to disguise what I write will be understood by anyone who finally succeeds in reading it. I don't want my thoughts to be read by the man in the street . . ."

Now I understood why the doctor had copied the quotation from the Gospel of John at the top of the second page: in order to draw attention to the fact that what followed were not Indian texts. He had taken every precaution to ensure that no layman should have the slightest inkling of the contents of the notebook: the same type of notebook as all the rest, the usual serial number, the same Sanskrit writing . . .

I was so excited that I didn't dare read any further. It was already quite late, and in a few minutes I would have to leave. If I had called Mrs. Zerlendi and read to her what was in the notebook, I might be acting contrary to the wishes of the writer. I would have to decipher it myself first, before disclosing the contents to anyone else. But I would not have time to finish it that evening, I told myself dejectedly.

Just then the door from the parlor opened and the housemaid came in. She seemed more sullen than usual, and her gaze was harsher. When I saw her approaching, I turned my eyes to the notebook, which I had opened at random. What I read there literally made me suffer at the thought that I couldn't stay there alone for a few hours without interruption, to find out all that had happened.

"Tomorrow and the next day we're cleaning house," said the housemaid. "So I came to tell you. I didn't want you to come all the way for nothing. Because once I start housecleaning, I don't finish for two days."

I nodded my head and thanked her. But the maid must have felt like talking. She came closer to the desk and pointed to the notebooks.

"All this infernal stuff will drive you out of your mind," she said emphatically. "It would be better if you told my mistress you can't make head nor tail out of it; you're missing out on the joys of youth, more's the pity . . ."

I raised my eyes from the notebook and looked at her searchingly.

"It was the ruin of the doctor," she continued.

"Is he dead?" I asked quickly.

"He ran off and met his end," she repeated in the same tone.

"But did you see his body?" I insisted.

"No one saw his body, but he met his end out in the wide world, without a candle at his deathbed . . . And he left this house a desert . . . Don't listen to my mistress," she added, lowering her voice. "She's not in her right mind either, poor thing. You see, two years later her brother met his end too, after coming here with a Frenchman, a French scholar . . ."

"Hans," I said.

"No, young master Hans came later. And he wasn't French either. He came afterwards, after the war. And he died too, young as he was."

I didn't know what to say. I looked at her in silence. At that moment I too felt myself enthralled by a strange enchantment I never had felt before. The maid ran the palm of her hand along the edge of the desk.

"That's what I came for," she said finally, "to tell you we'll be cleaning for a couple of days."

Then she left and disappeared, limping, through the same door, the one that led into the parlor. I looked down at the notebook again. I couldn't bear the thought of parting with it just now, right after I had found it, and not coming back for three days. Almost without realizing what I was doing, I took it and hid it under my jacket, trembling in all my limbs. I lingered a few minutes longer, until my agitated breathing had become normal again; I put away the rest of the notebooks, and then left on tiptoes, so as not to run into anyone who might guess my thoughts and my guilt.

5.

THAT evening I locked myself in as soon as I got home; I kept
the curtains drawn, to be sure that the light from my lamp
would not encourage any of my friends to disturb my solitude.
And as the night wore on, time and space around me seemed to
dissolve more and more into a turbulent mist, so overwhelmed
was I in my entire being as I deciphered Dr. Zerlendi's notes
page by page. And reading them wasn't easy. At first the doctor
had taken pains to write as carefully as possible, since it is difficult
to represent all the sounds of Rumanian with Sanskrit characters. But after the first few pages the transcription became more
and more haphazard, so that you had to guess at the words
rather than read them. Whether because of the excitement with
which he recorded his startling experiences in the notebook or
because of his great haste, Dr. Zerlendi's handwriting did not
make for rapid reading. In time the sentences became more and
more abbreviated and the words more and more technical, so
that it resembled a secret language or a code. On the threshold
of his final experiments the doctor had taken pains to preserve
his secret by employing yogic terminology exclusively, terminology which must remain largely incomprehensible to all who have

not, like him, delved deep in this science so rich in esoteric mysteries.

"Honigberger's letter to J. E. was for me the most complete confirmation," wrote the doctor at the beginning of his secret journal, but without saying who J. E. was or what was the contents of that letter, a letter Mrs. Zerlendi had alluded to in vague terms in one of our conversations. "As early as the spring of 1907 I began to think that everything Honigberger had written in his Indian memoirs was not only authentic in the strict sense of the word, but that it represented only a tiny part of what he had seen and what he had been able to perform himself." There follows a number of references to Honigberger's works: cases of "fakirism," levitation, suspended animation, live burial, and so forth, facts he felt justified in considering authentic. "I began my first experiments on the 1st of July, 1907. Some weeks earlier I had undertaken a serious examination of conscience, and had given up tobacco, alcohol, meat, coffee, tea, and all the rest. I won't try to retell here the story of this painful preliminary stage, which lasted six months. It took an iron will on my part, for many times I was ready to give it all up and return to my historiographic diversions. Fortunately Honigberger's letters proved to me that these things *can be accomplished,* and that repeatedly gave me new courage. I never would have imagined, though, that one could get so far, and with so little effort, relatively. For only after you acquire the first *powers* and the scales suddenly fall from your eyes do you realize how very great is men's ignorance, and how painful is the illusion by which they are taken in day after day, right up to the threshold of death. The will and energy a man devotes to satisfying his social ambition or his intellectual vanity is perhaps even greater than that which is needed to perform this extraordinary task: your own deliverance from futility, from ignorance, and from suffering."

96

The doctor describes in considerable detail—on that 10th of January, 1908, and the following days—his first experiments. As far as I am able to make out, he was familiar with yogic literature even before this, especially Patanjali's treatise and the commentaries on it, and he was acquainted with Indian ascetic and mystical philosophy—but he had never before tried to practice their teachings. He proceeded at once, it would appear, to that difficult experiment of rhythmic breathing, *pranayama,* but for a long time without achieving any encouraging results.

"On 25 July I fell asleep during one such exercise," he notes, after mentioning that a few days earlier he had been overcome by a coughing fit of unusual violence. "For a long time I did these exercises after midnight, and then early in the morning. A terrible sense of oppression in the chest and attacks of dry coughing were the only results. I realized, after two weeks of such efforts, that I was getting nowhere because, while practicing rhythmic breathing according to Patanjali's text, I was forgetting to concentrate my mind on a single object. The resistance I encountered was due precisely to this vacuity of mind, to which until then I had given no thought. Once again I tried following Honigberger's advice. I stopped my ears with wax, and began *pranayama* only after a few minutes of prayer. I reached a state of unusual mental calm. I recall even now those first sensations: I seemed to be in the midst of a raging sea, which gradually became calmer before my eyes, until nothing remained but a limitless sheet of water, without a single wave, without even the slightest tremor. Then came a feeling of abundance, which I can compare with nothing except the feeling that sometimes comes over you after listening to a lot of Mozart. For several days running I repeated the same experiment, but didn't succeed in getting any further. I would awake after a quarter of an hour in a state of vague reverie, though I knew that was not what the

97

result of the exercise was supposed to be. Somewhere along the way I had lost control; I had allowed myself to succumb to the spell which my own mind had cast round about me. I ran through the exercise once again, but after some time had passed the result was the same: reverie, sleepiness, or an incomparable mental calm . . ."

What a responsive chord was touched in me when I read this account! I too had at one time tried some of the experiments which the doctor had kept at so doggedly, and I had encountered the same difficulties. But he had been more fortunate, or had at least had a firmer will. During the first part of September, 1907, he made, almost without realizing it himself, a great step forward in the rhythmic-breathing exercises; that is, he succeeded in making the periods of inhalation and exhalation exactly the same length. "I began, as usual, by holding my breath for twelve seconds." That means that he took twelve seconds to breathe the air in, held his breath for twelve seconds, and breathed the air out again in the same number of seconds. "The object of my meditation that day was fire." No doubt he had "fixed" his mind on a basin of glowing coals, trying to grasp the essence of "fire," to discover this fire throughout the entire cosmos, at the same time absorbing its "principle," identifying it in the many different processes of his own body, and relating the infinity of fiery processes which together go to make up the universe and every organism individually to that very glowing element there before his eyes.

"I really don't know how it happened, but after some time I *woke up sleeping,* or, more precisely, I woke up in *sleep,* without having fallen asleep in the true sense of the word. My body and all my senses sank into deeper and deeper sleep, but my mind didn't interrupt its activity for a single instant. Everything in me had fallen asleep except the clarity of consciousness. I

98

continued to meditate on fire, at the same time becoming aware, in some obscure way, that the world around me was completely changed, and that if I interrupted my concentration for a single instant, I too would quite naturally become part of this world, which was the world of sleep . . ."

As Dr. Zerlendi himself later came to realize, on that day he had successfully taken the first and perhaps the most difficult step of the course he had decided on. He had achieved what is called in technical terms continuity of consciousness—passing from the consciousness of the waking state to the consciousness of the sleeping state without a break of any sort. The consciousness of the ordinary man is brutally cut off by sleep; no one maintains the continuity of his stream of consciousness when he falls asleep, no one knows that he is asleep (at most he may sometimes realize that he is dreaming), and no one continues to think lucidly in his sleep. From the world of sleep he remembers only a few dreams and a certain indefinable fright.

"What frightened me the most in this discovery of mine—that I was *awake* in my *sleep*—was the feeling that the world around me was completely changed and no longer in any way resembled the world of everyday consciousness. It is very difficult for me to define just how I perceived this transformation, for my whole mind was focused, like a single beam, on fire, and my senses were asleep. However, I seemed to be in a different kind of space, where it is not necessary to look in order to see—and I *saw* the room I was in gradually changing, the things, the shapes, the colors. All that happened on that occasion is beyond the power of description; nevertheless I will attempt to describe it, to the best of my ability, since no one, so far as I know, has ever dared to put in writing any such experience. I gazed unwaveringly at the fire, though not as a means of inducing a hypnotic trance; I have studied hypnotism sufficiently to know its technique and its effects. At the same time that I was gazing at the fire, I was thinking about it, I was *absorbing* it, penetrating with my mind into my own body, identifying all instances of combustion within it. Consequently it was not a static thought, but rather an integrated thought process, that is, it was not scattered in all directions, was not attracted by many different objects, was not distracted by any external stimulus or by any memory projected in a sudden burst from the subconscious. For this *integrated* thought process the fire was only a fulcrum, but by its aid I was able to penetrate everywhere that fire was to be found. Thus hypnosis was completely excluded, especially since I maintained uninterrupted clarity of consciousness; I knew who I was, why I found myself in such a position, why I was breathing rhythmically, and for what purpose I was meditating on fire.

"And yet, I was at the same time aware that I was in a different space, a different world. I no longer felt my body at all, only a vague warmth in my head, and this too disappeared in time. *Things* seemed to be constantly flowing, yet without changing their shape very much. At first you would have said you were seeing everything as if through turbulent water—but the comparison is not at all exact. Things actually were flowing, some more slowly, others very rapidly, but it would be impossible to say *where* they were flowing or by what miraculous process their substance was not consumed by this pouring out beyond their natural limits; though, to try to give a more exact account of my vision, it wasn't really a question of pouring out *beyond* the limits of an object, but rather that these limits themselves seemed to be constantly flowing. What was even stranger, all these things kept approaching and receding from each other involuntarily. Although I wasn't looking at them—of course I knew what was there: a pallet, two chairs, a rug, a picture, a night table, etc.—I had the impression that they would all gather in a single spot if I were to turn my eyes on any one of them. This impression was not a fancy, an illusion; it could be compared quite precisely with the feeling that a man has when he is in the water, that he can either go further into the water, or else come out of it. It was something that I knew, without being able to say whether I had ever experienced it before. Similarly I had the impression that I could look much farther than the walls of my room permitted. I wouldn't say that things had become transparent. On the contrary, apart from their constant flowing and their curious mobility, by which it seemed they would respond to any possible wish of mine to look at them, things remained just as they were before. And yet I could look out beyond them, although, I repeat, I had not tried to look. And it was decidedly not a case of looking *through* them, but rather *beyond* them. They were there right before my eyes, and yet I know that I could see farther, while they remained in their places. This feeling somewhat resembled the view of his whole house that a man can have from the corner of one room: he doesn't see through the walls, and yet he sees everything that he knows to be in the next room or in the whole house, without having the sensation that his glance has penetrated the walls."

6.

THERE can be no doubt that the doctor wrote all this only after he had had the experience of continuity of consciousness in sleep many times. From the legibility of the writing in this fragment it would appear that he composed the above account with great care and then transcribed it in Sanskrit letters—something he did not do later on, when he contented himself with making notes directly in the notebook.

"After some time I experienced the desire to penetrate deeper into the world of sleep and to explore that unknown space around me. I didn't dare, however, to take my eyes off the basin of glowing coals. A strange disquiet, I might even say a hint of dread, hung over me. I don't know what suddenly made me close my eyes; in any case it wasn't weariness, since, I repeat, I felt that I was asleep, yet my mind was more awake than ever. I was astounded to behold, with my eyelids closed, the very same scene as I had with my eyes open. Only the glowing coals seemed to have changed; they too were *flowing,* just like all the other things around them, while their glow was more powerful, though, I might say, much less *alive.* After a few moments of hesitation I opened my eyes again. I discovered that it wasn't necessary for me to *look,* to turn my pupils towards a particular corner of the room; I saw in any direction I wanted to, I saw wherever I turned my thoughts, whether or not I had my eyes open. I thought of the garden in back of the house, and in the same instant I saw it, just as if I had been there. What an amazing spectacle! It seemed to be an ocean of plant sap in ceaseless agitation. The trees were almost embracing each other, the grass seemed to be quivering like clumps of algae; only the fruit was quieter, seeming to be borne on a slow undulation . . .

"The next instant this vision of agitated plant life suddenly disappeared. I had thought of Sophie, and at once I saw her, in the big bed in our bedroom, asleep. Around her head hovered a dark violet aura; her body appeared to be continually moulting, so many folds were pouring forth from her, disappearing as soon as they detached themselves from her limbs. For a long time I gazed at her intently, trying to comprehend what was going on. Then I noticed a flickering flame glimmering now over her heart, now lower down, over her stomach. Suddenly I became aware that Sophie was beside me. It was a terrifying moment, for I very clearly saw her in bed asleep, and at the same time I saw her right there next to me, looking straight at me in amazement, as if she wanted to ask me something. Her face betrayed an astonishment beyond words; perhaps I looked different from the way she expected to see me, or perhaps I wasn't like the people she had met in her dreams up to that time. For only later, after repeating this experiment many times, did I come to realize that the figures I saw all around me were the projection of the consciousness of various people during sleep." (I must admit that I don't know what Dr. Zerlendi meant by this. I have, however, let this passage stand, because of the possible interest it may have for occultists. A *sadhu* with whom I spent some time in Konarak in 1930 told me—though

103

I'm not sure whether he was speaking the truth—that it was disturbing to encounter, in the course of certain yogic meditations, the spirits of people who are asleep, who wander around as shades in the dimension of sleep. You might say they look at you uneasily, unable to understand how it is possible for them to meet you, *there*, fully conscious and awake.) "A few moments later the space around me suddenly changed. Fright had returned me to the waking state again. I remained for some time in the same position I had been in since starting the experiment, and counted the seconds once more; my breathing rhythm had remained the same, twelve seconds . . ."

The return from dream consciousness to waking consciousness was a brutal one; the continuity had been interrupted by fright. Only after further experiments, carried out the next day in complete secrecy, did the doctor succeed in returning to everyday consciousness without the slightest break, by a simple act of the will. The words he used for this act of the will were: "Now I am returning." At the same time he reduced the rhythm of his breathing from twelve seconds to eight, withdrawing slowly from the sleeping state.

Concerning the experiments which followed next the notes are more abbreviated, whether because the doctor didn't want to say any more or because he wasn't able to—couldn't find any adequate description. Thus he declares at one point: "The unification of consciousness is attained by means of a *continuous* transition, that is, one without a hiatus of any sort, from the waking state to the state of dreaming sleep, then to that of dreamless sleep, and finally to the cataleptic state." The unification of these four states, which (paradoxical though it may seem) presupposes the unification of consciousness with the subconscious and the unconscious, the gradual illumination of the dark and impenetrable zones of psycho-mental life, is, in fact, the goal of the preliminary yoga techniques.

(All the Indian ascetics that I have known who have consented to give me any explanations regarded this stage, the unification of the states of consciousness, as the most important of all. Anyone who did not succeed in experiencing this could never derive any spiritual benefit from following yoga practices.)

Concerning the transition from the state of dreaming sleep to the state of deep sleep without dreams I find very few details. "I have succeeded in letting still more time pass between exhalation and inhalation: some fifteen seconds for each phase, occasionally reaching twenty seconds." This means that he was breathing only once a minute, for he held his breath for twenty seconds, took twenty seconds to inhale, and twenty to exhale. "I got the impression that I was entering a spectral world where all I saw was colors, which were almost without form. Or rather, spots of color. Furthermore, the world of forms was subordinated to the universe of sound. Every bright spot was a sound source." As far as I am able to understand, the doctor is trying to convey —in a few terse lines—some idea of the cosmos of sound, to which the initiate only begins to gain access after repeated meditations on the sounds, those "mystic syllables" of which the treatises on mantra yoga speak. It would seem, in fact, that beyond a certain level of consciousness you encounter nothing but sounds and colors, forms properly speaking disappearing as if by magic. But Dr. Zerlendi's description is too vague for us to be able to reconstruct his experience in detail.

The more startling the results of the yoga techniques become, the more reticent he is in telling about them. Concerning his attainment of the state of catalepsy he has only this to say: "With my last experiment I have acquired the ability to read the

105

thoughts of any person on whom I concentrate my attention. I was able to verify this with Sophie, who just at that time was finishing a letter to our overseer. Of course I could have read the letter directly, but I didn't; I was there beside her, and I read all her thoughts—not just the ones she was putting down in the letter—quite naturally, just as if I had heard her speak."

Astounding as these experiences are, Dr. Zerlendi doesn't attach any great significance to them. "The same result can be achieved even without following any very rigorous ascetic practices, simply by the greatest mental concentration. Though I am well aware that modern men are no longer equal to any such mental exertion. They are fragmented, or in a continual state of impermanence. You don't employ asceticism in order to acquire these powers, but rather so that you won't fall prey to them. The exploration of unknown states of consciousness can prove so alluring that you run the risk of spending your life on it without ever reaching the end. It is a new world, but for all that it is still *a world*. If you content yourself with exploring it, without wishing to transcend it—just as you have endeavored to transcend the world of waking states—it is just as if you learned a new language and then set out to read all the books written in this language, giving up all idea of ever learning any other languages."

I am not quite sure what degree of technical proficiency the doctor had reached when he began writing his journal. Some twenty pages were written on the tenth, twelfth, and thirteenth days of January, 1908; they comprise a sort of brief reminder, for any possible reader, of the preliminary stages, without making clear, however, just how far these preliminaries extend. He frequently mentions the initials J. E. "I think this was J. E.'s fatal mistake," he writes in one place. "He didn't grasp the unreal nature of the phenomena which he had discovered in the spectral world. He thought that this represents the furthest limit that the human spirit can reach. He ascribed an absolute value to this experience, when actually he was still dealing only with phenomena. I believe his paralysis can be accounted for in this way. Honigberger was probably able to reactivate certain of his centers, but more than that he could not do. He was unable to cure him of amnesia." This is an obscure passage; probably J. E. was unable to maintain consciousness to the very end, and so fell prey to his own discoveries in the supranormal world. I recall that all the Indian occult treatises speak of the new cosmic levels which the ascetic reaches through yoga techniques as being just as "illusory" as the cosmos to which everyone has access in his normal condition. On the other hand, I am not sure whether the "centers" he refers to are nerve centers or the occult plexuses known to yoga and the other traditions.

In any case, it would appear that this J. E., under the direct influence of Honigberger, had attempted an initiation of the yoga type, and had suffered a frightful fiasco, whether for the reason surmised by Dr. Zerlendi or because his constitution was unsuited to the techniques he wished to employ.

"I was successful in this," the doctor notes further on, referring to a complicated and rather mysterious experience of projection of the consciousness outside of the body, achieved in a state of catalepsy, "because I was, by way of exception, in an Asiatic sensory condition. I don't believe that normally a European can succeed in this. He doesn't *feel* his body below the diaphragm, and even feeling the diaphragm is a rather rare occurrence. Ordinarily he feels only his head; of that I am now convinced. I see them as they have never seen themselves, and not one of them can conceal anything from me."

This passage is rather cryptic. I presume that "an Asiatic sensory condition" could refer to the diffuse sensation that people have of their own bodies, which differs from race to race. I know, for example, that an Oriental feels his body in a different way from us Europeans. If anyone touches the foot or shoulder of an Oriental, he has the same sense of violation that we have when someone brushes our eyes or lips with his hand. As for "feeling the body below the diaphragm," this expression would refer to Westerners' inability to have a total *experience* of their bodies. In fact, very few of us can claim that we *feel* our bodies as *wholes*. Most people feel, properly speaking, only certain parts—the forehead, the heart—and even these only under certain conditions. Try to feel your feet, for example, in a position of complete rest, say stretched out on a bed, and you will see how difficult it is.

"I found it quite easy to unite the two currents, right down to the heels," the doctor writes further, in connection with the same experiment. "At that moment I had the very strong sensation that I was spherical, that I had become an impenetrable and completely impermeable globe. A comprehensive feeling of autonomy and invulnerability. The myths about the primal man, which represent him in the shape of a sphere, derive quite naturally from this experience of the unification of the currents." I wouldn't go so far as to say that this refers to the negative and positive currents of European occult therapeutics. It is more likely that the doctor had in mind the two fluids of the Indian occult tradition, "currents" which run all through the human body, and which according to yogic and tantric teachings correspond to the moon and the sun. I must emphasize, however, that I wouldn't dare to assert anything too positively, since I have only a fragmentary acquaintance with the stages of initiation he went through.

7.

Dr. Zerlendi's notes become more infrequent during the months of February, March, and April of 1908. The few pages written during this period are extremely cryptic, and they are devoted primarily to earlier experiences. The doctor's interest in his secret journal diminishes appreciably. Where at first he took pains to describe an experience as completely as possible, before long his interest in this task now fell off. Perhaps he recognized how incomprehensible such things must be to any uninitiated reader into whose hands the notebook might fall. Or perhaps he had already withdrawn from our world too far, and no longer had any interest at all in leaving an exact record of his experiences. In any case, during this period he almost never reports his experiences or thoughts of the time of writing. He keeps coming back to the events of the preceding days or weeks. I take it that his personal involvement with his discoveries was too great for him to write them down day by day. Especially when he undertook a new experiment he was so wrapped up in it that he didn't write about it until long afterwards, and then for the most part only very sketchily. "Uncertain results when I practiced *muktāsana* at dawn," he notes in April. It would

109

take several pages to explain this cryptic remark, which refers to a certain body position. I will therefore not attempt to explain it, for in Dr. Zerlendi's notes there are many such technical indications relating to the body positions assumed during yogic meditation, to breathing exercises, or to ascetic physiology. Furthermore, I have given some account of such practices in my book on yoga, so I won't repeat them here.

At the end of April, 1908, he seems to have taken a new interest in the journal. After the hasty and technical entries just preceding, there follows this long account. "Among other things of the highest significance which Honigberger revealed to J. E. was the existence of Shambala, that wondrous land which, according to tradition, lies somewhere to the north of India, and which can be entered only by initiates. Before he became insane J. E. believed that this invisible realm might after all be accessible to the uninitiated, and among his papers that I saw in Iassy I found one on which he had noted the names of two Jesuits, Estevão Cacella and João Cabral, who he claimed had reached Shambala. After considerable difficulty I have managed to obtain the works of these two Jesuit missionaries, but I determined that J. E.'s assertions were unfounded. Cacella and Cabral were, it is true, the first Europeans to have heard of Shambala and to mention it. While they were in Bhutan searching for the road to Cathay, they learned of the existence of this wondrous realm, which the natives believed to lie somewhere to the north. And they did set out in search of it, in 1627, but got only as far as Tibet. They never did find the wondrous land of Shambala. Unlike J. E., when I first read what Honigberger had to say about it I immediately realized that it cannot be identified with any region precisely locatable geographically somewhere in the heart of Asia. Perhaps I was partly influenced in this conviction of mine by the Indian legends of Agarttha, and also of the 'White

Islands' of Buddhist and Brahmanic mythology. I have, in fact, never come across any Indian text which stated that it was possible to reach these wondrous regions in any other way than by means of supernatural powers. All accounts speak of the 'flight' of Buddha or other initiates to these regions hidden from profane eyes. Now it is a known fact that in symbolic and secret language 'flight' is the term used to refer to man's capacity to transcend the world of the senses and thus to gain access to the invisible worlds. Everything that I knew about Honigberger led me to believe that he had succeeded in reaching Shambala thanks to his yogic techniques, in which he had become a master even before 1858, but that he had probably been unable to carry out successfully the mission with which he had been entrusted. That is the only way I can account for the fact that he returned from India so quickly, and why he died so soon after his return, leaving a document of such great importance in the hands of such a stupid young man as J. E. . . ."

How wildly my heart beat when I read the above pages! How many memories suddenly swept over me when I saw those two names: Shambala, Agarttha! For I too had once set out in search of the invisible realm. An old wound which I had thought long since healed over began to bleed again, recalling to my mind the months I spent in the Himalayas, very close to the Tibetan border, on the sacred road to Badrinath, making my way from one hermit to another and asking them whether they had ever heard of Shambala, whether they didn't perhaps know of someone who had learned its secret. And who knows whether in the end, in my hut on the left bank of the Ganges, in that *kutiar* half swallowed up by the jungle, which I have long thought of as a lost paradise—who knows whether I might not have found the answer right there, and after years of preparation and endeavor have succeeded at last in finding the way to

111

the invisible realm. But it was written that I was never to set foot there, but to bear within me to my dying day the longing for it . . .

How bitter are the regrets of one who has turned back in his course, only to learn later from someone else that the road he had set out on was the right one! Dr. Zerlendi's account confirmed all my surmises, for everything that followed took place exactly the way I envisaged it *must* happen to anyone who seeks Shambala with all his heart. "Always vivid in my mind was the image of the invisible realm which Honigberger had reached. I knew, of course, that this realm is *invisible* only to the eyes of the ordinary man. To put it more precisely, what this meant was that this land was inaccessible geographically, that you could only discover it, that is, after a rigorous preliminary spiritual training. I pictured this Shambala as being hidden from other men not by any sort of natural obstacles, by high mountains or deep waters, but by the very *space* in which it exists, a space qualitatively different from ordinary space. My first experiments with yoga confirmed me in this belief, for I came to realize how different the space of everyday experience is from the space of the other forms of human perception. I had even commenced a detailed description of these experiences in this present notebook, but I very quickly recognized that they are indescribable. Anyone who is familiar with them will agree with me. I continued with these notes nevertheless, because it is necessary that from time to time there should be a confirmation of the ancient truth, in which no one nowadays any longer believes. Honigberger himself, I now believe, had been permitted to return from Shambala in order to attempt the reactivation of a number of centers of initiation in the West which had been inoperative ever since the Middle Ages. His sudden death confirmed me in this belief; I have no doubt that he either didn't know how to fulfill his mission, or that his attempt was a failure right from the start; that is why he died in such a mysterious way. As for myself, while I haven't yet achieved any conclusive results, I believe I can sense an invisible influence being exerted on me by someone who is guiding me and helping me, and that strengthens my conviction that I shall in the end succeed."

Dr. Zerlendi says no more concerning this invisible influence. Occult tradition, however, has a good deal to say about it, especially oriental tradition; and all that followed leads me to believe that the doctor was laboring under no illusion when he mentioned it. For his progress in yoga proceeds very rapidly, with almost dizzying speed. The summer of 1908 he spent alone on one of his estates, and later, after returning to Bucharest, he summarized some of his experiences. Some of these can be reconstructed with a degree of assurance. For example, he spoke in one place of the strange vision he had after certain meditations; it seemed to him that he saw everything upside down, or to be more precise, exactly opposite to the way things appear in reality. For instance, hard objects seemed soft to him, and vice versa; "emptiness" impressed him as being "full," while solid matter seemed to him insubstantial. But there was another thing about which Dr. Zerlendi gave no precise details at all: he saw the whole world in its entirety—to quote from his manuscript—"exactly opposite to the way it appears to a person in the waking state." He doesn't explain what he understands by the expression "exactly opposite." But this much is certain: we are dealing here with an expression which is in agreement with the strict formulas of the mystics and the books of ritual, for texts of this kind constantly speak of the other world, the world known in ecstasy, as being "exactly opposite" to the one we see with our physical eyes.

Equally strange was the doctor's account of the "return" to the visible world after a prolonged period of contemplation. "At first I had the impression that I was tottering, that I would fall down at the first step. I no longer had my normal assurance, as though it were necessary for me to readjust to three-dimensional space. Consequently it was a long time before I dared to move at all. I remained there motionless, waiting for a miracle to occur to restore to me the assurance I had before falling into trance. Now I can understand why after an experience of ecstasy saints remain for hours or even entire days without moving, giving the impression that their spirits are still enraptured with the divine."

On the 11th of September he noted: "Several times I have tried cataleptic trance, the first time for twelve hours, the second and third times for thirty-six hours. I told the forester I was going to the manor house; I locked myself into my room alone, knowing that I would not be disturbed. For the first time I was able to verify personally the experience of *stepping out of time*. For although my spirit remained active, my body was no longer participating in the passage of time. Before going into trance, I shaved, and after thirty-six hours my face was just as smooth as at the moment I fell into trance. And it was only natural that this should be the case. For *time* is experienced by man through the rhythm of his breathing. For every man a certain number of seconds elapses between inhalation and exhalation; *life* coincides, in man, with *time*. The first time I went into cataleptic trance at ten in the morning and came out of it at ten in the evening; during this entire time my body was lying in what some have called suspended animation, without drawing a single breath. The inhalation of air at ten in the morning, that is, was followed by the exhalation at ten in the evening. During that whole interval my body was withdrawn from the passage of time. For my body the twelve hours were reduced to a few seconds—the long inhalation in the morning, and the slow ex-

114

halation preceding my awakening. On that day I lived, as a human being, only half a day; in twenty-four hours my body aged only twelve hours; life was suspended, but my organism suffered no harm as a result."

The experiment Dr. Zerlendi had undertaken is common enough, as a matter of fact, but to this day it has never been adequately studied. "Suspended animation," which caused such a sensation in Honigberger's day, really does appear to be a stepping out of time. That is the only possible explanation for the fact that after a trance of ten or even a hundred days the body has not lost any weight and the newly-shaven face remains as smooth as before. But these are states which categorically transcend the human condition, and we can form no conception of them at all. Even the wildest imagination cannot adequately grasp such a "stepping out of time." The references we find in the confessions of certain saints or in oriental occult writings are unintelligible for all of us. I myself have assembled a valuable collection of such accounts, most of them expressed allegorically, but they have remained for me mysteries sealed with seven seals. For some of us only death will cast a new light on this problem.

"To me the only remarkable thing in all this is that people learn nothing from such demonstrations. The most noted of scholars have contented themselves with denying the authenticity of these happenings—even though hundreds of witnesses have been present when they occurred—and have preferred to maintain their old positions. Just as if you were content to cross water only by swimming, thus giving up all thought of crossing the sea, simply because you do not believe it possible that water can also be crossed by boat."

115

8.

In September, 1908, the journal breaks off for five months. The entries which follow next are from the beginning of January, 1909. Because of their technical nature I cannot reproduce them here. They are for the most part merely statements of metaphysical principles and practical instructions for yoga. Some of them seem to make no sense whatsoever. "26 January: the experience of darkness. Every letter taken up again from the beginning." No doubt this refers to other earlier exercises, probably to meditations on sounds and letters—the so-called *mantra yoga*—although I have found no account of this. But what can he have meant by "the experience of darkness"? And later: "5 February: Recently I have experienced *samyama* over the body. It is unbelievable, *and yet it is true.*" This note makes sense if the doctor is referring to a certain text of Patanjali, which says that through *samyama* over his own body the yogi can make himself invisible to the eyes of other people. (*Samyama* is the term used by Patanjali for the last three stages of yogic development, which I cannot discuss here.) I find it difficult to believe, however, that the doctor had experienced this wonder as early as February, 1909. For then how can I explain his surprise at a later date? How can I explain the eighteen months that followed, during which—although he tells us very little about it—we nevertheless know that he was constantly trying to acquire this very power of making himself invisible?

Moreover, the difficulties with the text constantly increase. Some entries seem quite contradictory. "15 March: Took up some of the Upanishads again. Astounding progress in understanding the original." How am I to understand *this?* After all that he had already achieved, reading the Upanishads in the original was no great feat. And then, what significance could this study of the Sanskrit language possibly hold for a man who had reached a degree of spiritual understanding far more valuable than any scholarly learning? Unless perhaps he had turned back in his course, or failed to advance in his practice of yoga, under an "influence" of which he says nothing. Or perhaps he was no longer engaged in scholarly study, reading the text and analyzing it; perhaps instead, as they say all over India, he had succeeded in attaining a mysterious knowledge simply by reciting the sacred words, which are considered there to be a revelation of the Logos, paying strict attention to their exact pronunciation. As a matter of fact, elsewhere he mentions certain exercises—of which the exact nature remains a puzzle—of the "inner recitation" of a sacred Indian text. And at the beginning of the summer he speaks of the correspondence between the "mystical letters" and certain states of rarefied consciousness (I would come closer to the truth if I simply said "superconsciousness").

During this same period he speaks of the "occult vision" which he acquired by "reactivating the eye between the eyebrows," the eye of which Asiatic mythologies and mystics also speak, which is said to confer on its possessor the ability to see to immense distances. Concerning this "eye of Shiva," as the Indians call it, there are, to be sure, conflicting reports, or at least reports which are extremely obscure to the uninitiated. Some say that this "eye of Shiva" is directed towards ordinary space, and would thus be a sixth sense; others, and they are in the majority, assert that the new vision which the initiate acquires through this "eye" has nothing to do with the world of forms and illusions, but is concerned exclusively with the spiritual world. With the "eye of Shiva" man can observe the spiritual world directly, that is, he has access to supersensory levels. But Dr. Zerlendi has nothing specific to say about this mystery either. Is this because he couldn't, or because he didn't want to?

Again there follows a long interval of silence; I am unable to determine its limits, as the entries immediately following are not dated. And these entries, furthermore, are all but indecipherable. I surmise that they refer to what Dr. Zerlendi called "impersonal consciousness," since the following passage is included among them: "The thing most difficult to achieve, or perhaps even impossible to achieve nowadays in the West, is impersonal consciousness. In recent centuries only a few mystics have ever attained this state of consciousness. All the difficulties that man encounters after death, all the hells and purgatories in which, we are told, the spirits of the dead are tormented, are due solely to this inability to achieve impersonal consciousness while they are still alive. The tragedy of the soul after death and the frightful purifications it undergoes are nothing but the stages of the painful transition from personal consciousness to impersonal consciousness . . ."

The page immediately following the above entry had been torn out of the notebook. Then I found an entry dated 7 January, 1910. "Perhaps I have been punished for my impatience. But I took the view that you are allowed to create your own destiny. I am not so young any more. I have no fear of death; I know only too well that the thread of my life will not be spun out for

118

very much longer. But I felt obliged to try and hurry, for I am no longer of any use to anyone here where I am, while I still have a great deal to learn *over there.*"

A few days later: "I now know the way to Shambala. I know how to get there. And there's something more I can say: three men from our continent have very recently succeeded in going there. Two of them, it is true, are Russians. Each one set out alone and reached Shambala on his own. The Dutchman even traveled as far as Colombo under his own name. I know all these things from my long trances, when I see Shambala in all its glory, when I see that green wonder amid the snow-covered mountains, those quaint houses, those ageless men who speak to each other so little, yet who understand each other's thoughts so well. If it were not for them, who are praying and deliberating for everyone else, our whole continent would have been convulsed by all the demonic forces which the world has unleashed since the Renaissance. Is the fate of our Europe really sealed, then? Can nothing more be done for this world, prey to dark spiritual forces, which are hurrying it all unknowing along the road to cataclysm? I very much fear that Europe will meet the fate of Atlantis, that it will very soon be destroyed by sinking beneath the waves. If men but knew that it is only thanks to the spiritual forces emanating from Shambala that the tragic shifting of the earth's axis, so well known to geology, is again and again averted, a shifting which will cause our world to be submerged in the depths, and I know not what new continent to emerge . . ."

The fear of a tragic end for our continent is expressed on other pages of the journal as well. I get the impression that the doctor was beginning to see more and more clearly the series of cataclysms which were to burst over Europe.

This view is in agreement, by the way, with a whole series of prophecies, more or less apocalyptic in nature, concerning *Kali-*

119

yuga, the "dark age" whose end, we are told, we are approaching with rapid steps. All over Asia legends are in circulation about the imminent end of our present world, though they differ greatly from each other in form. Dr. Zerlendi, however, mentions a possible "shifting of the earth's axis" as the immediate cause of the disaster. As far as I am able to understand, such a shifting of the axis would, according to him, set off a tremendous seismic catastrophe, in which some continents would be submerged or would change their shape, while new continents would emerge from the sea. The fact that he several times mentions the name of Atlantis leads me to believe that he considered the existence of this continent to be a reality, and that he connected its disappearance with some sort of spiritual degeneracy of its inhabitants. What seems to me most worth emphasizing in all these tragic predictions is the fact that they were made several years before the First World War, at a time when the world was still cradled in the illusion of unending progress.

And then suddenly, on the 11th of May, 1910, he returned once more to the yogic exercises through which one can achieve the invisibility of the body. For readily understandable reasons I will not reproduce here these astounding revelations. A strange feeling of panic seized me when I read these lines of Dr. Zerlendi's. There had come to my attention up to that time numbers of documents, more or less authentic, which dealt with this yogic miracle, but never before had I seen the facts stated so plainly and in such detail. When I began the present account, I was still vacillating, uncertain whether or not I really ought to include this horrifying page. Now that I have got this far, after so many weeks of indecision and worry, I realize that things of this sort cannot be revealed. I am consoled by the thought that those who know what is meant by *"samyama* over one's own body" will also know where to turn for further information about it.

120

9.

I would appear, however, that experimenting with invisibility was not without its dangers. The effort required to make his body invisible to the sight of others, to *withdraw* it from the light, caused such a shock to his entire system that after one such experiment the doctor lay unconscious for several hours. "I shall probably not resort to this means of getting to Shambala," he noted in June, 1910. "The time of my final departure is approaching, but I still don't know whether I shall have power sufficient to make myself invisible to the others when I leave."

Later that same month: "Sometimes I too seem to be afraid of the forces that I have concentrated in myself. My will never wavers, but I find it quite difficult to control all these forces which have, up until now, helped me to enter the invisible worlds. This morning, while I was locked in my room in a state of contemplation, I all at once felt the atmosphere become rarefied, while my body suffered a drastic loss of weight. Without wanting to, I was slowly rising, and although I tried to hang on to the things in the room, I shortly felt my head touch the ceiling. The frightening thing about this incident is that the levitation occurred against my will, solely because of the forces unloosed

121

by my contemplation. I had almost lost control, and a single moment of inattention would have caused me to plummet to the floor."

I have heard of other cases of similar strange occurrences, when someone who is attempting to gain mastery over occult powers finds himself unable, at a certain point, to maintain his clarity of consciousness and his firmness of will, and thus runs the risk of falling prey to those very magical forces which his own meditation has released. I was told in Hardwar that the most terrible dangers await the yogi not at the beginning of his training, but at the end, when he achieves mastery over deadly forces. Likewise, in the world of myths we are told that those who have "fallen" the lowest were the very ones who had succeeded in approaching the divine most closely. Satanic pride, too, is a form of the dark forces which you release as a result of your own development, and which in the end may succeed in destroying you.

Later, on the sixteenth day of August: "A terrible sense of detachment from the whole world. Nevertheless, there is a single thought that still thrills me: Shambala. I don't plan to make any sort of preparations before leaving. I made my will the year Smaranda was born. Any other indication now, on the eve of my departure, would only arouse suspicion."

Then, perhaps later the same day, a few lines set down in haste: "It has occurred to me that perhaps after all this notebook could fall into the hands of someone who might destroy it, never suspecting what it contains. In that case my efforts to leave a record of some extraordinary events will have been in vain. But I have no regrets . . ." Following this a whole line has been crossed out, but I have been able to decipher part of it. "If anyone who reads and understands . . . should try to make any use of . . . serious . . . will not be believed." Evidently the doctor, on the eve of his departure, had thought of leaving some advice for any possible reader, at the same time warning him of the risks he would run if he should be so foolish as to consider publishing the notebook. I have no idea what made him change his mind and cross out the sentence he had already started. I have, however, respected his wishes by not divulging his most remarkable experience.

"19 August: I woke up invisible again, and my alarm was all the greater because I had done nothing to bring about this condition. I walked around the yard for hours, and only discovered by accident that I was invisible. The servants passed by without seeing me; at first I thought they were too busy to pay any attention to me, but then I looked around and found I couldn't see my shadow. I followed one of the farmhands on his way to the stables. He seemed to sense something evil behind him, for he kept looking back with uneasy glances, and finally he quickened his pace and crossed himself. Despite my best efforts, I was quite unable to make myself visible again before midnight, when I woke up on my bed exhausted. The unparalleled weariness that followed was, I think, due particularly to my efforts to become visible again. For it had taken no effort on my part to become invisible—it had happened by accident; I had no intention of doing it, and indeed wasn't even aware of it . . ."

This is the last entry of any length in the doctor's journal. What follows, however, is no less spine-tingling: "12 September: Since the night before last I have no longer been able to return. I have taken this notebook and a pencil, and am writing this sitting on the stairs that go up to the attic. Afterwards I shall hide it among my exercise notebooks. I am seized with fright at the thought that I might fail to find the way to Shambala after all . . ."

This entry is dated *two days after the doctor's disappearance.* If anyone at that time had been able to decipher the manuscript and had read this freshly-written page, he would have realized that the doctor was still in the house, very close to his family . . .

10.

On the third day I went back to S. Street, determined to return the notebook and to read it in its entirety to Mrs. Zerlendi. I was met by the old housemaid. Her mistress was ill, she told me, and the young lady had left for Paris.

"But why did she leave all of a sudden like that?" I asked in surprise.

"That's the way she is when she makes up her mind," she answered, avoiding my glance.

It was clear that she was not going to tell me anything more. I gave her my visiting card, saying that I would stop by in a few days to inquire after her mistress's health. But I was unable to get back there until a week later. The entrance gate was locked, and only after I had shaken it several times and had rung the bell in vain did the housemaid finally come out to meet me. With difficulty she made her way across the garden, in which the last flowers seemed to have faded overnight, and approached the gate, muttering to herself.

"Madame has gone to the country," she said, and was about to go back to the house.

But she stopped again to add: "She didn't say when she'll be back."

Several times that autumn and winter I returned to that gate on S. Street, but always found it locked. At best I was told: "There's nobody home." But sometimes the housemaid didn't even bother to come out to speak to me.

Then I wrote Mrs. Zerlendi several letters, but I never received any answer, or even any acknowledgment that she had opened my letters. I couldn't imagine what had happened. Mrs. Zerlendi had absolutely no way of knowing that I had found her husband's journal and had taken it with me. I was certain that no one had seen me hide it under my jacket. Even if someone had been looking through the keyhole to spy on me, he still couldn't have seen anything, for when I took the notebook I was in the far corner of the library, with the rest of the doctor's exercise notebooks all around me.

Towards the end of February, 1935, I again passed by the house on S. Street, and finding the gate open, I went in. I must admit that it was with considerable agitation that I rang the bell at the vestibule door. I expected the same sullen old woman to come to the door, but to my surprise a young servant girl let me in. I asked whether anyone was home. "Everybody's home," she replied. I gave her my visiting card and went into the parlor. A few minutes later the door from the bedroom opened and Smaranda appeared. I would hardly have recognised her: she looked ten years younger, she was attractively made up, and her hair was a different color. She glanced at my visiting card once more in surprise before giving me her hand. She put on a fine pretense of not recognizing me. And she pronounced my name as if she had never heard it before.

"To what do I owe the honor of this visit?" she asked.

I told her that I had spent some time working in Dr. Zerlendi's library, and that her mother knew me quite well—it was she, indeed, who had invited me to go through her husband's papers —and I added that I also knew her, Smaranda.

"I'm afraid you must be laboring under a misapprehension," she replied with a smile. "I am quite sure I have never met you before. As a matter of fact, I know very few people here in Bucharest, and I would certainly have remembered your name, or at least your face . . ."

"Nevertheless, Mrs. Zerlendi knows me quite well," I insisted. "For weeks on end I worked right here in the library." And I motioned towards the massive oak door.

Smaranda followed my gesture, then looked at me in surprise, as though she couldn't believe her ears.

"What you tell me is very strange," she said, "for this really is where my father had his library at one time. But that was many years ago, a great many years ago. During the occupation that library, which was an unusually fine one, was broken up . . ."

I began to laugh, as I didn't know what to say.

"I find it very difficult to believe what you are telling me," I finally answered, after a long pause, during which I looked her straight in the eye, to give her to understand that I saw through her little game. "Scarcely two months have passed since I was working in this library. I know it shelf by shelf, and without going in I can describe for you everything that is in it."

I would have continued, but Smaranda hastened to the door of the bedroom and called, "Mother, do come here for a minute!"

Mrs. Zerlendi appeared, holding a little boy by the hand. I bowed deeply, but I could see in her eyes that she didn't want to recognize me.

"The gentleman claims that he worked in the 'library' two months ago," said Smaranda, motioning towards the massive oak door.

Mrs. Zerlendi looked at me with offended surprise; then she stroked the child's head and whispered, "Hans, you go and play."

"Didn't you yourself write to invite me to come, and weren't you the one who took me into the library?" I began in exasperation. "Why, you asked me to continue the biography of Dr. Honigberger, which your husband had started," I went on.

Mrs. Zerlendi looked in surprise from me to Smaranda. I must admit that she played her part well, and I felt the blood rise to my cheeks.

"It is true that my first husband, Dr. Zerlendi, was working on the life of some Transylvanian doctor, but I confess, my dear sir, that I no longer remember his name very well. Twenty-five years have passed since the death of my first husband, and since the war the library no longer exists . . ."

I stood there dumbfounded and couldn't take my eyes off the door, the door I had so often opened, and only two months ago at that. Seeing my astonishment, Mrs. Zerlendi added, "Smaranda, show the gentleman the room!"

I followed her as if in a dream, and stopped on the threshold bewildered when I saw the new appearance of the library. Only the chandeliers and the curtains were still there. The desk, the shelves of books, the big carpet, everything had disappeared. That huge room was now a kind of living room, with two tea tables, several sofas, a bridge table, and a number of fur rugs in front of the fireplace. Where the library had been was now only faded wallpaper, partly hidden by pictures and old weapons. The wooden gallery which had run around three of the walls had disappeared. I closed the door, bewildered.

"You are right," I said, "the library is gone. If only I knew who had bought it," I continued. "I would have liked to learn more about Honigberger . . ."

"But my dear sir," said Mrs. Zerlendi, "the library was broken up nearly twenty years ago now."

128

"But the most significant thing is the fact that you don't recognize me," I said with a smile.

It appeared to me that Mrs. Zerlendi's hand trembled slightly, but I cannot be certain of it.

"Our amazement is even greater than yours," began Smaranda. "It is decidedly strange that someone should know the room in which there was a library twenty years ago, a room which, as I well know, very few outsiders have entered in recent years . . ."

I was getting ready to leave. I realized that for reasons unknown to me neither one of them was willing to recognize me. Had they been prompted to act thus by some invisible influence coming from the other side?

"I wonder whether the old lame housemaid, as least, would know me? I spoke with her several times just a few weeks ago," I added.

Mrs. Zerlendi turned abruptly to Smaranda.

"He means Arnica!" she whispered in fright.

"But Arnica died fifteen years ago!" exclaimed Smaranda. "How could he have seen her a few weeks ago . . ."

I felt my mind reeling and my vision blurring. If I had lingered a few minutes more, I would have collapsed senseless right there at their feet. I murmured a few words of excuse and left, scarcely daring to raise my eyes. Only after I had wandered through the streets for a long time and had come to my senses again did I get a glimmer of understanding of this strange turn of events. But I have not dared to confide my ideas to anyone, and I shall not reveal them here either. My life was unsettled enough as a result of the mysteries Mrs. Zerlendi had asked me to investigate, without knowing what solution the doctor had found . . .

A few months after the events narrated above, I happened to be walking along S. Street again. The house at No. 17 was being torn down. The ironwork fence had been partly demolished, and the pool was filled with scrap iron and flagstones. For a long time I stood there watching, in hopes of catching sight of one of the two women, or of finding out something which might throw light on their unaccountable behavior. But there was no one but the workmen and a contractor who was supervising them. Afterwards I continued along the street, weighed down with this mystery, which I was quite unable to fathom.

Ahead of me I thought I caught sight of the little boy who had come into the parlor with Mrs. Zerlendi. I called to him.

"Hans," I said, "am I ever glad to see you, Hans!"

The child looked at me with carefully feigned surprise.

"My name isn't Hans," he answered very politely. "It's Stephen."

And he continued on his way, without looking around. He walked slowly, like a child whose only worry is that he can't find any of his playmates.